THE WATCH

THE WATCH

S T O R I E S

RICK BASS

W. W. Norton & Company

NEW YORK   LONDON

Acknowledgments

Acknowledgment is made to the publications in which these stories first appeared: "Juggernaut" and "The Watch" in *The Quarterly;* "Mexico" in *Antaeus;* "Choteau" in *GQ;* "Mississippi" in *Cimarron Review;* "The Government Bears" in *The Southern Review;* "Wild Horses" in *The Paris Review;* "Cats and Students, Bubbles and Abysses" in *Carolina Quarterly;* and "Redfish" in *Esquire.* "The Watch" has been selected for *New Stories from the South 1988* and *Prize Stories 1989: the O. Henry Awards.* "Cats and Students, Bubbles and Abysses" has been reprinted in *Best American Short Stories 1988.*

Particularly helpful advice has been given by Carol Houck Smith, Tom Jenks, Rust Hills and Gordon Lish on several of these stories. The author also wishes to express his grateful acknowledgment to James Linville and the staff of *The Paris Review* for their encouragement on all of the stories.

Published simultaneously in Canada by Penguin Books Canada Ltd.,
2801 John Street, Markham, Ontario L3R 1B4.
Printed in the United States of America.

The text of this book is composed in 11/14 Avanta,
with display type set in Bauer Text Initials.
Composition and manufacturing by The Haddon Craftsmen, Inc.
Book design by Margaret M. Wagner.

FIRST EDITION

Library of Congress Cataloging-in-Publication Data
Bass, Rick, 1958–
The watch.
I. Title.
PS3552.A8213W3   1989   813'.54   88–12543

ISBN 0-393-02623-X

W. W. Norton & Company, Inc.
500 Fifth Avenue, New York, N. Y. 10110
W. W. Norton & Company Ltd.
37 Great Russell Street, London WC1B 3NU
1 2 3 4 5 6 7 8 9 0

For
Timothy Schaffner
and
Carol Houck Smith

CONTENTS

THE   WATCH

MEXICO

~⌣~

*K*irby's faithful. He's loyal: Kirby has fidelity. He has one wife,
Tricia. The bass's name is Shack. The fish is not in an aquarium.
It's in the swimming pool that Kirby built, out in his and Tricia's
front yard.

It's a big pool. I believe it can hold a twenty-three pounder.
When we're drunk, I'm sure of it. That sweet suck of lime: the
beer, so cold. Some way you have got to get by in Houston these
days. Hell will come here first, when it opens. Everyone here's
already dead. The heat killed them or something. People don't
even fall in love here anymore: it's just the pelvic thrust, and
occasionally children as the result. There's no love, and that's the
surest sign of death.

Kirby paddles around in his scuba gear and watches Shack;
makes sure she doesn't construct any plans about leaving, slipping
off somehow to the bayou, which calls from nearby. Shack is a
Florida hybrid, the kind that can put on two or three pounds a
year. Tricia's from a warm climate too. I'm a neighbor—Kirby's
best, and only, friend—and the pool is deep. You wouldn't believe
me if I told you how deep.

Kirby sprinkled stumps, gravel, old trees, down into the pool
for structure. Kirby's volatile. When his old Volkswagen broke,

fuel injectors yet again, he pushed the whole car into the clear water. It floated down like a blue heavy bubble: it bounced in slow motion when it landed. Shack lives down in the backseat now. Shack is a female, of course; they grow faster and larger, and are more aggressive. I help Kirby guard the pool from the neighborhood kids fishing it. Word got out. It's hard to tell, but it looks like she'll go about eight or nine pounds already. Kirby bought her for a dollar from a fish hatchery three years ago. She was six inches long, thin, like a cigar.

"That one," he said, pointing into the sea of fingerlings that was moving away from us wherever we followed, shifting and flowing back the other way in the big tank. The boy with the net was perplexed.

"That one," Kirby said. "I want that one." This, three years ago. He picked a good one.

Tricia lies out by the pool in her swimsuit with her buddies. They drink Corona beer and margaritas, and wear their sunglasses. Houston presses down. Being Southern ladies, they can't tan. They just get wetter and wetter, sweating the beer out, and they get hotter and hotter, sometimes managing to turn an attractive, even luscious shade of pink, like the sweet part of meat deep up inside a crab's or a lobster's claws. None of Tricia's girlfriends will go swimming, not even for a dip, no matter how hot it gets—a hundred, a hundred and three—because they know the fish is in there, and that it is a big one. They've never seen the fish. It's just the idea, something big being down there below them that they can't see, that frightens them. I can understand.

Even Tricia won't go in, not even with Kirby, and Tricia's different. Tricia goes to the bullfights in Nuevo Laredo with us, and she doesn't turn back from them, doesn't turn away. In fact, she loves them.

She wears her sundress, one of many, and tilts her big sunglasses up over her hair, which is the color of good wheat, and up in the stadium, at these bullfights, she'll rise to her feet. We'll have been drinking margaritas all day until we're as limp as puppets, and she'll stand up and cup her hands, while Kirby and I sit on the bleachers and sway, trying to focus on what is happening down in the arena with bloodshot eyes that hurt to look.

"Kill him," she shouts; she's screaming. It's an affront, the way that bull refuses to die. The brave man in the center: the animal threatening his existence, challenging him. *"Kill him!"* she screams, turning red in the face, the sun, the heat, the blood drying in the sand, the margaritas. Kirby and I look at her, mortified, too drunk to talk, but-it's-just-a-bull, Tricia, please sit down . . . but we don't ever attempt to calm her, to ask her to please sit down. You can't control some things, and that's what makes them the best. We love to go to the bullfights with Tricia.

She doesn't let up; and the people sitting all around us, it's just a Sunday afternoon, something to do, but they start to get caught up in her excitement, and they're rising to their feet too, shouting things in Spanish now, applauding the matador, looking over at Tricia, applauding her red face, her shrill American cries—and it is more fun for Kirby and me to watch her than the fights themselves, and Kirby and I sit on either side of her and look up at her, and we marvel.

W̶hen it rains, when the floodwaters lap around the edges of the pool, Kirby turns on the underwater floodlights situated around the perimeter at various depths, as in a regular swimming pool, and the three of us, and any of the neighborhood kids who can be trusted, circle around and around, barefooted and in our shorts, slapping the top of the water with bamboo poles, keeping Shack at bay. We don't want her to get too curious and realize there's a way out. It doesn't flood often; Kirby's and Tricia's house is on the largest hill on the street, a wonderful imperial wooded knob, but if the storm is sudden enough, it can happen. The underwater lights shoot fuzzy beams from all directions across the pool, like a submerged Hollywood opening, solid beams of spinning underwater mote debris, through which Shack's large dark shadow sometimes passes, moving slowly, caudal fins spinning, deep below, looking up as if judging: it's definitely a competition. The record is twenty-two pounds and four ounces, and that was fifty years ago.

The outdoor magazines say such a fish would be worth a million dollars. Kirby is foolish enough to believe them, and Tricia, lovely enough. I'm just along for the ride: to see if it can be done. It is like the beer commercial, the one that says you-can-have-it-all ("Yes!" cries the chorus). Kirby and Tricia want to move to Eagle Pass, down on the border, and build a castle with the money. I'd be sad to see them go. Kirby bought me the house I live in: loaned me the money for it, rather. They've been married three years, and as best as I can tell, have gotten all the fighting out of their system. They really love each other. I like to see that.

We go to Mexico, so often. We know that drive; we know which flights leave, and when. Sometimes we'll take the train down there, and drink all the way down. If anything gets even a little out of sync—a hangnail, an obscene phone call, the appearance of chinch bugs in the yard across the street—we head for Mexico.

Gus fishes Kirby's pool some nights. It's like a Greek tragedy; I'm bound in the inexorable whorl, the clash of the triangle. There's nothing I can do. Gus claims to have hooked Shack often.

"I'm on to what she likes," he says. He snaps his dirty fingers. "Yellow crankbaits, with a pork rind trailer, dipped in horse urine; I can catch her, just like *that.*" The reason his fingers are always dirty is from the various odd jobs, his strong money greed, and he has trouble snapping them. He tries and tries; then gets it. Poor Gus. Kirby has fired on Gus before: rained heavy-grained bullets used normally only for deer hunting into Gus's old truck, popping out the windshield once, hitting the gas tank another time, though it did not explode. Gus driving quickly and without his fishing tackle into the night. Kirby, in his underwear, Tricia in her robe. Lights up and down the street.

"They were trying to steal SHACK!" he shouts into the night, an explanation to the neighbors. And they know, or think, that Kirby is pure bluster, and the lights go back off, and Tricia takes the gun from him, steers him back into the house—he wants to don his scuba gear and turn on the underwater lights and check right away, go search for his fish—but somehow Tricia gets him into the house, and we all settle back in, to the night, in our homes, to our sleep, in the darkness.

Gus and Kirby and I used to be roommates, before Tricia. Money is strong; it can assemble almost anything, do everything. We lived in a trailer in one of those camps with crushed-shell drives clustering out from one central power facility/post-of-fice-box center. We all plugged in to this one light pole, and rent, once we had split it three ways, was $45 a month. It was dark in that shell of a trailer, and Kirby and I came to hate just the sight of Gus's face, because he was happy. He had big glasses and a horse-ass smile, and was always rubbing his hands together. Kirby didn't have Tricia then, as I've mentioned, not yet, and I was miserable too, just because I was still young then, hadn't yet outgrown my unhappiness, and we grew to hate Gus more and more, like the buzz of a fly that cannot be seen but is in the room. Gus was in our lives.

Gus had money too, which made us hate him more. All his fucking jobs: and all he did with his money was spend it. He was always ordering things off of the TV, ordering pizzas delivered to our trailer. If you could buy any sort of service, pay someone to do something for you—anything—Gus would give money, spend, to have someone give him something: anything. He couldn't get enough.

He dialed those places in Florida where they talk dirty to you: a girl telling you what she wants to do to you—though I suppose there was a number you could dial and have a guy come on the line instead. What I'm saying is that Gus had money and that was all, and his soul was dead and we hated him even more because he had the option of *not* living in that trailer. He could have bought a house in town with a cool garden, and shade, and a breakfast room window. Sun, and wind chimes with their tinkle. He lived in the trailer instead, because he liked living with us. We were in that dark hell for four years: 208 weeks.

I don't want to hear any of that old song about how it couldn't have been *that* bad. I don't want to hear it. I've got a nice house, three houses down from Kirby's, on the same street. If you want to know, it's far and away one of the nicest streets in Houston. My house cost $325,000; Kirby's more. If I pay Kirby $5,000 a year, I can have it paid for in sixty-five years. I'm a little behind, already.

It's near the bayou, where we live. There are tall pine trees. When you drive in at night, back late from dinner, there are rabbits on the lawns in the moonlight. There's some rich sons of bitches that live out here: so rich, so secure, that they don't even need to be offended, or threatened, by Kirby and me, by the pool, by Tricia drinking margaritas in the front yard in her swimsuit. That's how nice it is.

We got out of college, and for graduation Kirby's grandfather gave Kirby a bunch—about a hundred—of little oil wells that he'd accumulated over the years, just throw-away things that he had, sprinkled all throughout the state: slow, toy pumpers, almost make-believe in their movements—stripper wells that Mr. Simmons had been carrying for tax purposes. But instead of Kirby's living off the rather comfortable monthly production checks from all these wells, as Mr. Simmons had no doubt pleasantly and responsibly visualized, Kirby turned right around and sold them, when reserves were going for $42 a barrel on the spot market, for cold cash, every last one of them. One of the wells had something funny happen to it—a recompletion, they called it—and was suddenly worth many hundreds of times more than what they thought it was—and Kirby, with this great wash of money, fled the trailer, left Gus, and bought the house back in the trees in which he now lives, and he bought me the house I live in, too, while both of us were still breathing hard, in our flight from Gus. Also, that's when he built the pool.

So I don't want anyone to think that Gus wasn't bad. It was like being in a coffin, like being tied up in a plastic garbage bag with rotten meat, and dead things, the stuff that comes out from beneath your teeth when you floss after sleeping all night, and we'd never been that close to such a thing before: didn't even know it existed. I'm so glad Kirby got the oil.

Gus had a dog for a while when we were first living with him: a girl dog that he called Bitch.

Maybe Gus's behavior and attitude toward women is what made us love them so much. Almost beyond reason. You've never seen anyone take care of someone the way Kirby looks after Tricia. If you think lending me the money for the house was nice, you should see how he treats Tricia. I think Kirby's good to us because both of us were just victims of Gus: me, through my college years; and Tricia because she was a woman.

Once when we were drunk and driving around in the country on a weekend, back in college, driving Gus's truck, which was still new, just driving through fields, scaring up meadowlarks, chasing them down the sides of hills, for a thing to do, Kirby told Gus that in Mexico, and all foreign countries, and even in certain parts of Houston, the way you told a girl you wanted to sleep with her—"to do it, Gus," Kirby said—was to throw pieces of banana at her. We told Gus the various sections of Houston in which to try this: that the newest thing in the city for girls on the make was to pretend to be waiting for a bus, at the bus stop.

"What they're really waiting for, Gus, my man," Kirby told him, "is bananas."

Meadowlarks leaped up in wild alarm, flew down the hills. We thundered across logs, over rocks, down into creek bottoms, chasing them as if they were butterflies, the truck bouncing and jolting. Gus driving: a wild thing, but dead. He didn't love.

*T*ricia has these wonderful earrings, pale blue, with silver in them, that go well with her blue eyes, and her smile, and her hair. Kirby got them for her on one of their trips down to Mexico. They hold hands a lot of the time, even in this, their fourth year. Kirby had known her less than a month when they married. There was a franticness about it that somehow made it more beautiful. Gus and I were in the wedding, and also a couple of Kirby's cousins, guys roughly our age, from down around Corpus Christi. It was a pretty odd assemblage. I mean, he just didn't *know* anybody. And he was selling those oil wells off hand over fist in those days, a new batch every day. Things were going fast. We were escaping, both of us, getting away. We didn't think, not then, that anything was following: that was how fast we were moving. We thought nothing could follow.

Tricia has this very nice Roman sort of nose, it looks good on a younger woman or even an older one, it makes her look imperious, but what I liked even better about Tricia—better than this imperiousness—was its opposite, her amazement, while all this stuff was going on: the wedding plans, the moving trucks, the whirl. Who *are* these people, Kirby? Shying away from Gus instinctively. The two cousins, Rocky and Jake, bull riders, cowboys from the coast with tans and mustaches. Cajun accents, somehow.

*T*here's a bar not four blocks away from our houses. You walk out to the interstate, from our woods, and it's on the frontage road: the Cadillac Bar and Grill, an Americanized version of the real one that's down in Nuevo Laredo. People go to this one for lunch in the day, and after work for drinks. Work. Kirby and I laugh at them.

They serve Corona beer there. It's hard to get: the Mexican National Brewery only made seven thousand cases this year (last year they only made three thousand). It's the In beer, now, in Houston. You're supposed to be seen drinking Corona. Also it tastes good, it seems to get colder than other beers—the thickness of the bottles, I think. This bar on the frontage road, the pseudo-Cadillac, has lots of Corona. Kirby and I walk home, clawing through people's yards, swinging at the shrubbery, falling to our knees, getting up, struggling home, breathing heavily from the beer: that Houston sweat of night. Kirby's big house up in the trees, with the floodlights, is like a tabernacle, a state capitol. It's like the last hole on a golf course: the clubhouse.

The smaller fish in the pool leap and play, chasing June bugs and moths all night. We're full of beer, and our hands are greasy from the nachos, or whatever they had that night. Finger enchiladas. The taco bar. We know Shack is down there.

Often we sit in the lawn chairs, back in the shadows, and watch the smaller fish: they are brave under the night lights. Bug heaven. Kirby squeezes one eye nearly shut, like a detective, and watches for the children to come sneaking up the lawn, with their fishing tackle. Once some of the teenagers in the neighborhood poured a can of gas into the pool and lit the slick; we were all in the house, playing Uno. We felt the thump of hot air jumping, even inside. It was like one of the Civil War movies when the powder room goes.

Fire trucks came and had to spray foam into the pool. It killed most of the fish. We knew it wouldn't kill Shack; she would be staying down in the VW, in the deep below the flames and the poisons. Fish like that can live to be fifteen, twenty years old. They're smart.

Around two in the morning, when we've had a good one at the Cadillac and are out in the lawn chairs, Tricia will bring cotton sheets out and drape them over us, so that we look like chairs in a museum, covered from the dust. Once when she did this Kirby woke up but kept his eyes shut, and then when she bent over him to cover him, he leaped up and yelled "Boo!" He loves her dearly, and they have their whole lives to spend together.

*T*he pool is low on minnows. We drive to a place Kirby knows, and seine minnows: hundreds of them, even thousands, thick and silver, leaping over the net like tiny salmon. Tricia sits on the hood of the car in her straw hat and watches. It's something to do. She's still moving forward. It's been three years, and I have to wonder if they ever talk about having children. It's none of my business to ask.

*T*he rehearsal dinner was up in the Petroleum Building, on the fortieth floor. We drank wine and wore our suits and Gus was awed by the beauty of Tricia, of the bridesmaids, and he behaved, and his teeth, in the light from all the candles, were yellow, and brown, and cracked. His eyes thought all the wrong things as he looked around at the peace, at the joy.

We went by the hotel afterward, where Kirby's bull-riding cousins were staying, to change out of our suits. To go to all the naked breast palaces. They were all in safe neighborhoods, the people who went to these things often wore ties, it was really amazing. Watching a film for the bachelor party would have been too lonely, too abject: the small screen, the sense of enclosure, in somebody's house. Tricia tried to lock Kirby with a variety of doe-eyed looks of concern as we left the rehearsal dinner but it was dark and they didn't carry the message that she wanted them to, I don't think. He couldn't really see her that well, and we were hurrying out.

We ran for our cars and after quick consultation decided to all ram Gus's truck at once, from all directions, on the great empty width of late-night Main Street beneath the tall street lamps, and I still and always will remember Gus's grinning, manic face, our headlights reflecting off his moon-glasses, when he realized what was happening as we began turning our cars around, loops and squealing turns and circles, and headed back, converging on him. Someone was going to give him something.

We knocked him silly, hit him from four directions at once, and with force. We couldn't have been drunker. Gus rolled out of his truck and fell to the street, laughing tears, holding himself he was laughing so hard. Rocky screamed and jumped out of his truck and with his bare hands and kicks of his boots pulled Gus's bent hood off the frame and hurled it noisily into the street. Tricia watched from the lobby with her hand over her mouth.

It was just the beginning.

We went into Caligula's, stunned at first by the noise and flash of lights—and not by the women's nakedness, or dancing, but by their smiles: they were truly happy. In fact, they were delighted; we'd never seen such exhilaration, such happy faces. We stood there and watched. A girl came and took us to a table. Her breasts were riding our elbows as she steered us through the crowd, she was touching us with them. Her nipples looked broad and like something we'd never seen before that close, and in that context. It was her face, her mouth, that we wanted to watch, though; there were plenty of breasts, all uncovered and all around us, with lights and motion—the noise, though, was what was so overpowering, and it made talk, and words, the rarest thing, the thing we wanted. We leaned closer to her, trying to hear what she was saying.

There's a false satiety that sets in in these places, but then the weight of its falseness, after a while, suddenly presses down and sharpens the hunger that was thought to be gone. We kept going outside where we could hear each other talk, and also just to keep reexperiencing the pleasure of coming back in.

It seemed cool and fresh whenever we went back outside: it was invigorating.

On about our third trip outside—Gus's big glasses fogging up, coming out of the building's air conditioning—a short sweating black girl in a purple wool miniskirt, barefooted, calves and thighs like a linebacker's, approached us from nowhere, stopped halfway to us, then motioned us to the parking lot. She had warts on her face and on her arms.

She was so ugly, so spellbinding, that we had to follow.

She reached her car, an old copper-colored Ford Galaxie, with three other girls still in it, waiting—the engine was running, idling, for some reason—and the girls inside were all as dark as the night itself. She turned and put her hands behind her back, on the handle of the car door, and we could see her teeth moving, like semaphore, as she spoke. She was the ugliest woman on the face of the earth. Our town had created her. She was ours.

"Ten dollar," she said.

Gus pulled out his wallet and began counting. It was hard to believe.

*I*t was taking forever. We looked out at the car. We could just see her head moving under the street light; Gus's face was back in the shadows of the car and we couldn't see him, and were glad, though we had to look.

We went back in to watch the girls. They ran and jumped and did cheers, and slid up and down poles, wrapped their legs around them and mated with them. There must have been over a hundred of them. You think your girl's breasts are the best in the world, just because they're unique, and then you see a couple hundred of them at once, not any of them at all alike, and you know you are right, but in a lesser way. A bachelor party is a thing to survive, like so much else. I don't think that other thing, with a girl in the back room, the girl without a face, just her legs up for you, is done any more. Too dangerous; too dangerous!

We ordered the god-awfully expensive drinks, and watched the girls, and waited for Gus to come back in. Maybe, we thought hopefully, they were robbing him.

Mostly it's just drinking. Driving cars into each other, head-on, at twenty, thirty miles an hour, on empty, lamplit Main Street: the gold light coming down past the oaks, twinkling, spilling like haze at a football stadium. The crunch and tear of metal, the tinkle of glass, the laughs and cheers. Seeing who can make the biggest noise.

I don't know if this is a fact or not but in college a tame professor I had once, a real nerd, pushed his glasses up higher on his nose and told me, aiming the whole lecture at only me, it seemed—he stared at me the whole time, looking at no one else, and this was a large class—about this one species, which, it turned out, is kind of ridiculed in scientific circles because, according to the fossil record, this inept dinosaur was only able to cling to the earth for six million years, while even the most ignorant, backward, brainless sorts were lasting twenty, thirty, one hundred fifty million years. I can't remember the professor's name either.

I think it was that dinosaur that was half bird and half reptile, one of those first ones to leap out of trees, thinking it could fly. The professor was laughing while he was telling us all this, picturing the scaled thing, eyes bright, scrabbling up a tree; going out on a limb, crouching and leaping, maybe trying to catch a wind current. Leaving the tree, and then striking the rocks, breaking itself. The thing didn't have a mind, a brain; just a feeling. God knows *what* was in it that kept urging the species to do that, repeatedly. Climb the trees and leap. Trying to leave its environment, I guess, before times got tough. Which it did manage to do, in a way.

That's where you find all their fossils, too, or most of them: dozens and dozens, almost always in twisted shapes that are unnatural and broken, and painful even to look at, even trapped in old rock. You go out into the desert (said the professor) and in your dig, you try to find a fossil tree, the trunk of a big stout one, the equivalent, I suppose, of our live oaks today—a good *jumping* tree—and then from that, in your diggings, you radiate, work outward, and you start finding these little half-bird things, as many as you could ever care to collect. Half something, half another thing.

Gus came back in with the inner happiness we knew he'd have; it was more than just a smile. He was in love with life. He had had the O in the ugly girl's mouth. It made the girls sliding up and down on the poles suddenly seem like innocents, like maidens.

Wedding parties, bachelors: how does the bride, eventually—over the tenure of her term, the length of the marriage—finally get all the pieces and fragments of what went on? Why does it matter? The fear in their eyes; the *importance* of it, to them, of a thing missed. They get a snatch of it here, pick up a tidbit the year after that; sometimes there'll be a dinner party and great long stretches of the narrative will come out, after eleven-thirty, told charmingly, happily, among friends—Tricia will lean forward and be worried, she will be listening with concern . . .

You weren't trying to *leave* me, were you? Tricia's eyes will say whenever the bachelor party is mentioned, whenever anyone's is discussed. I'm the only thing that can hold you, her great wide eyes seem to say. I don't want you going up into any trees. She looks like a mother on these occasions, looking at her child: she's here to protect what matters. There'll be a white tablecloth and candles. Kirby will be leaning back, sated. King Kirby. He's always laughing, if he can help it. Something's always funny now in his life. He's found the right woman, and I don't know what she sees in him, what the purpose is, but she sees it.

*F*or some reason, I find Gus's truck frightening. He came out of it the worst, the night of the party and, unlike us, he didn't get his dents and crunches repaired, touched up or painted. He drives on with it the way it is, like some kind of barbarian, to whom nothing matters anymore. The hood was never put back on; when you ride with him, you can see pistons and everything.

"I'm going to catch that damn fish of Kirby's," he tells me. He says it like he's forgotten I'm Kirby's best friend. I don't know why I still go places with him occasionally. It's so sad. I can't bear to think of letting him know of my dread, of just the way he is. Gus isn't going to last long. It's like he has a cancer. It can happen to anyone; it's the least I can do. Still, when I'm riding with him, listening to him babble, I feel like I'm holding my breath. At least he won't last long. And I'm free; it's different from when I was in college.

The doves call so sweetly in our neighborhood, in Kirby's and mine. It is taking us no time at all to become snobs on how to live. It's happening easier than anything.

"Thanks for the ride, Gus," I tell him when he lets me out. I don't have a car. His tattered truck is shaking abjectly, like an old dog, and blue smoke is coming out of it from several places, as if through perforations, the kind you'd see in a block of Swiss cheese.

Gus looks grim and wild and alone, sweating behind his glasses, as wild as Rocky, as he prepares to go back to his trailer, his hovel, the one where we all used to be. He knows Kirby and Tricia and I go down to Mexico together all the time.

"Adios!" he cries, still grim, and roars off, the bomber, a ninety-mile drive ahead of him, smoke pouring from behind, as if he is mortally hit. A man so lonely. He wants to stay and try to change his life, to be a different, more accepted person. Maybe he wants to be Kirby. Maybe he wants to be me.

Kirby isn't home, and neither is Trish, so I put a note on their door and ask them to come over for margaritas if they get in soon enough. I go home and plug the blender in, get everything ready. But they don't show; they don't get in, I suppose, until late. They also have their own lives to live. We have all these distances set out before us, and we can do what we want with them, our lives. We are all in perfect and proper control. We can make happen what we want to happen, in our lives, and there is all the time in the world.

Sometimes I go for walks early in the morning. Some of the professional people are leaving in their black cars. Audis. Benzes. Quiet. Everyone in Houston in 1986 has tinted their windows a solid black. You can disappear inside. You can blow the air conditioner on 3-Maximum, and listen to whatever tape you want to, its chrominess hissing nicely, and look out at breasts, at faces, at women, at old men, at the ones who have only a few years left to be alive.

I walk barefooted and in my shorts, without a shirt, in the cool dust that collects in the street gutters from the rains and winds, and doves fly from high in the pines; sometimes a housewife will come out, down her walk to get the paper, and she will wave. I know I must look young to all of them. The sun in our neighborhood, our woods, is odd, because it is as orange in the early morning, coming through the fog, as it is at sunset, when it is going down behind all the heated particles of haze and smog. Such real beauty.

Sometimes, I'll walk by K's house. If he is out with Tricia by the pool, reading the papers, having a cup of coffee, sharing mirth over the price of oil while the city collapses, and he sees me and waves me up, I'll go up: sit and have a cup. Maybe swim some, a few easy laps and lazy, and have Tricia get me a towel. They've got the nicest towels: the cream color of luxury, wedding gifts, they weigh about five or six pounds each and are wickedly rough; you can really get dry, and feel ready to face the rigors of the day.

I like the way the water feels, too, when I get out of the pool, the way it slips down my calves, around and behind to the insides, down over the heels, splattering. Maybe I'm a sensualist, and no good at moving forward, at climbing those trees—or, rather, at *leaping*—maybe I'll never be able to go anywhere on my own or *do* anything—that's what a friend of Tricia's said, one horrible occasion when a double date was accidentally created—we went to a drive-in movie, if you can believe it: twenty-six years old, all of us, and our first, ever. There were mosquitoes, and the night was muggy, we had to roll the windows up and run the air conditioner, idle the engine, and just watch, without hearing the voices . . . we left after about thirty minutes and went to the

Cadillac and drank—that was when Tricia's friend so very help-
fully volunteered what was wrong with me—

—but there's time. You can learn from everybody else's mistakes; isn't that the best way? You can stay off the field, on the
sidelines, and spare yourself the crunch of gristle, crack of bone.

Shack catches most of her minnows, and her five-cent gold-
fish, in the deep. Rarely does she come to the surface. Just a bolt
of movement, green far below and large, and then back she goes,
into the car: a fish is gone, a shiner, a minnow; a sloppy, lazy
perch.

Maybe there will be a bad hatch of mosquitoes one day. A
thunderstorm. Perhaps the Astros lose. We go to Mexico. The
flights cost seventy-nine dollars, one way.

When we get there, Kirby loves to practice his Spanish. Sometimes, when he means to say to the cab driver, "Take me to the
bullfights," it will instead come out "I have a cat in my house"—
said with a great and mysterious pride, his eyes closed even, so
pleased is he with his mastery of the language—but we've got a
book too, and we're learning. This fall I may get a job down at
one of the nurseries, because I'll be running out of money, but
also because it would give me a good chance to learn the words:
working with Mexican laborers, aliens. It'll be embarrassing to
sweat so much, though. I've watched them, and none of them
sweat. They know, down in Mexico, how to work without getting
hot. They pace themselves. I've watched everything.

August. The hurricane season. We've been down in Laredo,
and Nuevo Laredo, for a week. We drove, this time, in Kirby's

jeep. We bet on the horses, on the dogs, and went to the bull-fights. We drank margaritas as often as we could stand it, and then some. We drove deep into the poor country, broken and cracked and roads turning to dust, children without clothes, a cantina only every thirty miles, and we bought Coronas for a quarter, a dime, then a nickel, as we got closer to the source. We lay out in the sun and sunbathed. It wasn't like our old lives, when we were in school, and with Gus: we were doing something. We had a good time and came back with many pounds of cheap Mexican coffee, all flavors, a lime squeezer, some piñatas, and cases and cases of Corona, smuggled: a simple blanket over them, there was no check.

It was different when we got back into Texas, we could tell that it was. We drove for great stretches, and didn't say much. Our faces and arms were as dark as animals'. Our lips were blistered—we drank a good deal of water. Whoever wasn't driving almost always slept. We drove 70, 75, 80 miles an hour.

It was dark when we reached Houston: there's no tiredness greater than that of driving all day, with a sunburn, after a vacation. The lights of the restaurants and streaming blurs of car headlights assaulted us, disoriented us. In Mexico, one of the matadors had gotten gored, twice: first in the calf, dropping and turning to reach for it, the pain; and then in his back. We saw the horn come out the other side. It appeared, the end of it a small thing, in his stomach. We drank a lot of beers that afternoon after the fights. We drank all we could. We wanted to know the language, so we could find out if he had lived.

*T*he lights were on at both our houses when we got in: we've got those automatic timers. We pulled up into Kirby's drive first, to check on Shack. I was going to help Kirby unload all the beer.

Tricia was going to go upstairs into the bedroom, into the air conditioning, to sleep: her head hurt.

There were some kids on the patio, by the pool, and they had fishing poles. The climbing turn of our headlights coming up the drive caught them, froze them like rabbits.

"Shit," Kirby said, and it was like the vacation had never happened. Even Tricia looked worried, for the fish. One of the kids, a big high school-sized one—dirty jeans and grubby cut-off sweat shirt, dark hair and a belly—had a stringer of fish. There were four other kids with him. They had to have been fishing all day, and perhaps all the night before that; there were a lot of fish on the stringer.

They ran down the hill, weaving in and out of the big pines. The oldest fucker, the big one, was carrying the stringer of fish, running with it like it was a string of firecrackers that was about to go off. Some of the fish were coming off the stringer as he ran; some of the other kids were dropping their tackle boxes and poles. By the glare of the streetlight, we saw one of them, the smallest— he could not have been more than nine years old—run smack into a tree. He was just looking back over his shoulder, up the hill at us, and then he went down, he just sank, and it was like the way the matador had gone down, the one that got gored. We passed him, kept running, after the big one, the one with the fish, who was into the center of the street and running down it like a small airplane taking off from a big runway: he was pulling away from us.

Far ahead of us, we saw him look back at us and drop the stringer—running, faster and faster, passing from concentric circle of light to light, past each distant street lamp, getting farther and farther away from us.

We stopped, gasping, when we got to the stringer of mostly dead fish. Shack was on it. A few of them, Shack included, were flopping weakly. But they had that bluish glaze starting up on their eyes, and they had all this street dust and gravel on their scales, and also up in the tender redness of their gills, and there wasn't any doubt that the only thing they were doing was hurting, that there wouldn't ever be any more life in them. They gasped the air, trying to get the other thing, but unable to find it: their mouths gaped, wilder and wilder, as if they'd been tricked. We were too far from the pool to do any good.

It's like Gus is a friend now, so bad were the children who caught and killed Shack. Kirby even invites him over. Tricia's sapped. She tried. She gathered everything and tried to hold it together. But she's loosening up too. We all drink together now, around the house, and sometimes we make jokes, and laugh, lightly.

She's just an old woman, now: thirty, thirty-one. But I remember when she was younger, and when Kirby laughed, really laughed. I remember her rising up in the stadium, too, down in Mexico, so far from home, and cupping her program in her hands like a megaphone, and shouting in the heat, "Kill! Kill!" as the matador feinted, and stepped back, and twisted, and turned to escape what was coming.

CHOTEAU

Galena Jim Ontz has two girlfriends and a key to Canada. It's the best hunting in North America, up the road, past the entry gate, where he has this key. The tiny dirt road going into Canada hugs a mountain face on one side, and the sheerest of cliffs on the other. Driving it, if you dare, you can look down and see the nauseating white spills of rapids in the Moyie River. There's not a dead-end sign or anything to warn you when you first get on this road, and you follow it straight up the mountain, around a few bends, then—as if climbing into the clouds—always, you keep going up, and the smart people who somehow find themselves on this road will stop and park, and get out and walk, if they want to see what's ahead (no place to turn around: you have to suck in your breath and back down, stopping to throw up sometimes— the jeep, or truck, slides when you tap the brakes, rolls on the loose gravel, acts as if it's going to take you over the edge and into space beyond; sometimes it does, and you can see wreckage on the rocks below). But Galena Jim guns his old black truck up the road without a care, and when he gets to the heavy crossbar gate with the padlock on it, no sign differentiating the United States from Canada, just a gate, he gets out and opens it with his key, and we drive through, and then he gets out again and locks it behind us, and we've left northern Idaho and are in a new country, pioneers, it seems, hunting in a country that has never been hunted.

"Oui," says Jim, grinning. He's got black hair, an old lined-looking face—he's forty—and light blue eyes, a kid's grin. "Oui, oui, oui." It's the only French he knows. He loves to hunt. I don't know how he got the key. Some sort of charm or guile somewhere, I'm sure. People only see that side of him. Though surely Patsy, who has been his girlfriend ever since she left Oklahoma with him, sees the other part. I do, too. He is still a boy, still learning to be a man, this in the fortieth year of his life. He doesn't always make the right choices—but he's still trying, he still has choices to make, at least—an odd, stubborn sort of purity. I like Patsy. She's forty, also. I'm not so wild about the girlfriend Jim keeps in Libby. The girl is sixteen, has yellow hair, and is a hard talker, ready to get out of the sticks, ready to go on the road. Except she's frightened, I think, and wants Jim to go with her. Which he won't, of course.

But he's got that choice. He still has so many! And who wouldn't want to have Jim Ontz, Galena Jimmy Ontz, on the road with them, that first time?

Everyone else sees just the boy in him, and is charmed, says, "That Jim," etc., chuckles, buys him a drink, or what-have-you, and they think that's how he is, that he's a wild man, the wild man of Yaak Valley, and are glad to have him, a legend living among them, like a damn motto or state flag or something.

They don't understand that he's still growing up, that he's just getting rid of things, and trying to keep other things out.

They call him Galena because of what he did to the road when he first moved up here, back when he and Patsy were about to get married. (They never did.)

It was about ten years ago, and they'd just made the big strike down near Thompsons Falls. Galena is usually found as an ore, mixed in with what they call "country rock"—and all sorts of processing and smashing and refining is necessary to separate it—but occasionally a vein of pure glittering space-blue slick and shiny heavy-as-lead galena will be discovered, and they can claw that directly out of the mountain with a bulldozer.

Jim had left the rodeo circuit, had come north. Most of the people living in the Yaak, then as well as now, were from Texas, but Jim was from Oklahoma, a little farther north. The country was and still is too tough for anyone else. It was when they were first putting a real road in through the valley—the last valley in the Rockies before you get up into Canada—and it's still the last valley in Montana without electricity, and probably always will be—and Jim was working on the road crew, helping cut and blade through rock and forest the little one-lane road that follows the Yaak River, which flows west into the Kootenai.

What Jim did was to steal a cement mixing truck from the road crew project, late on a Friday afternoon, after everyone had gone home—Jim was the only crew member who actually *lived* in the valley, all the others had gone home to Libby, or Bonner's Ferry, or even Eureka—and he took it down to Thompsons Falls, with me and Patsy along for company, and he backed it up to the roadside cut where they were mining all of this galena straight from the vein.

He climbed up on top of the mixer, so that he was right against the cliff, and with a hammer and railroad spike, he chiseled into the vein, spilling pebble- and cobble- and fist-sized pieces of galena down into the cement mixer's huge bowl. We held flashlights for him so that he could see, and whenever a lone car or truck would come driving down the road, we'd turn the flashlights off and hold our breath. Jim would keep chipping, though, banging away at the side of the mountain with savage, rooting swings, as if there was something *buried* beneath the galena.

It was a dark night, with the moon not up yet, but the galena was so shiny that it caught even the starlight, and Jim looked wild up there in the dark, his big arms and shoulders working frantically.

And when he finally had the mixer loaded the way he wanted it, half-and-half—it was about midnight—he climbed down, too tired to drive, and Patsy drove us back to Yaak, taking dirt roads, going up through canyons, cutting across meadows, taking all the shortcuts, skipping the few little towns between Thompsons Falls and Yaak. We got stuck in the last meadow outside of the valley, coming up along a dry little beaver-dam creek, and we had to dump some of the galena-and-cement to lighten our load.

By that time the moon was up over the mountains, and it shone down on us so brightly, lighting our every move, that it seemed unnatural, wrong—*too* bright—and as the galena splashed into the shallow creek, making a little dam, it sparkled with an eerie blue light that seemed almost to come from within, like some beautiful new electrified form of life, maybe even life being created, inside the mixer.

We got the big truck going again, and drove, sliding and groaning, all the way up through the pasture like that, leaving a wide trail of galena, as if some beautiful animal had been wounded and was leaving a glowing blue spoor.

When we got back out to the road, Jim hopped out and shut the sluice pipe, and no more galena was lost: but it's still out there, a hundred-yard stripe of it, and hunters call it Galena Meadows now instead of the old name, which was forgotten, and that's even how it shows up on the maps; and it's beautiful, in the moonlight, shining in the night like an electric blue blaze. Helicopters land on it, whenever they have to fly into the valley to pick up an emergency patient, because it's so easy to see, even in bad weather. The meadow is the safest place to land, and they aim for the galena, illuminated by their landing lights, shimmering, almost pulsing, as the winds blow snow across it.

What Jim did next was pretty self-incriminating.

He drove down the sidewalks of the little town of Yaak—a mercantile on one side of the street, and the Dirty Shame Saloon and a few houses on the other side—and with the cement mixer growling and tumbling, sloshing all that mixture around inside—lights coming on, from the cabins along the road—he poured galena sidewalks for the town, on either side of the new road that was coming through, and when he was finished with that he drove around and around in circles in the center of town, pouring a town plaza, right in the middle of where the road would be coming, so that it would have to fork left and right around this slick blue circle. And Dickie McIntire, the owner of the saloon, came out and with the snowplow on his truck graded and leveled both the sidewalks and the little plaza-circle, and by the time the sun was coming up, the men of Yaak were building a gazebo out of lodgepoles in the center of the large blue circle, and Jim and Patsy and I had returned the cement mixer and had gone home and were sleeping hard.

There aren't but twenty or so people living in the valley, and we all liked the new sidewalks and the new plaza, and felt they were at least what the road crew owed us for the inconvenience of the new road and the people it would bring—and so no one said anything on Jim, although he had poured a little strip of the galena mixture all the way up to his cabin before returning the mixer—and then, even after the crew started back to work on the road, working for several more weeks, bits and chunks of galena were still falling out of the shaker, being poured out onto the new road, and now, at night, in places all along the new Yaak River Road, your car or truck headlights will pick up sudden, flashing blue-bolt chunks and swatches in the road, blazing like blue eyes, sunk down in the road—the whole road glittering and bouncing with that weird blue galena light, if you are driving fast.

*J*im says you need two of everything up here. Winters hit forty, sometimes fifty below, and the air as still as your sleep. Two trucks, two chainsaws, two girlfriends, says Jim. Two axes, two winches, two sets of snow chains. Mauls, generators, cross-country skis: two of everything, depend on nothing, and he's right, of course.

I moved up here from Fort Worth twelve years ago, and have given up trying to live with a girlfriend or a wife. I've gone through three of them, and the partings have always been wild and bitter, never pretty, always leaving great relief on either side after it was over. It's a rough country, and beauty doesn't do well up here unless it's something permanent, like the mountains, or the river, or even the great forests, century-old larch and cedar. Jim and Patsy have been together as long as anyone up here, though, so perhaps what he says is true.

The mean hard-mouthed girl comes into town sometimes, for a drink at the Dirty Shame, and whenever she comes in, Patsy gets up and leaves. The mean girl from Libby is named Wilmer, but Jim and everyone else calls her Tiger. She just turned sixteen in the spring; she used to be fifteen when she first started coming up here. It's a different country.

I watch Patsy going out to the truck, walking proudly, not looking back, whenever Tiger shows up. I really like Patsy. Patsy might be the best thing in this valley. She tans Jim's hides and pelts, helps him with his trapline. She's got long brown hair, down almost all the way to her butt, and a good, strong face. She's from Illinois, but you'd swear Alaska. Patsy makes what she calls "dream hoops" for the entire valley, beautiful wreaths of bird feathers, feathers she's found and not killed to get—grouse, eagle, crow, jay, owl—and the wreaths are small and thick, spiraling in on themselves, all feathers, with only a finger-sized hole in the center.

You're supposed to hang them over your bed, she says, right over your head, and all the bad dreams that would otherwise come to you in the night, making you anxious and tense the next day, instead get tangled up in the birds' feathers. The good dreams are free then to come in through the small hole. It works, strangely enough; everyone agrees that it works. It's spooky.

Jim says that in the absolute dead of winter—during the Wolf Moon of January—trees splitting, exploding like fireworks all over the valley, and deer and elk freezing in their tracks, frozen in upright positions, standing out in the bright white meadows like statues, with no place left to go, just *frozen,* finally, from the great cold—he and Patsy will get so cabin-fevered, so out of their minds and rage-crazy that they could *kill* each other with swords, if they had to. When they start feeling that rumble coming on, that low, slow kick in the back of their heads and between their ears—the itch starting up—then one of them will go lock the guns in the barn and throw the key into a snowdrift, where it will not be found until spring thaw; and then, when their hate for each other, and for everything, for the entrapment of the cabin, can no longer be stood, but when stepping outside might be fatal—lung-searing, at a wind chill of seventy below—they put on these huge red inflatable child's boxing gloves—"Rocky Boppers," they are called—and with these monstrously-oversized balloon-fisted gloves, they'll stand in front of the fire and just let each other have it, whaling away, pounding and pounding on each other, jabs and hooks and uppercuts, all of it, fighting for over an hour sometimes, fighting until they can't stand up; collapsing then, exhausted, as if drunk, in front of the fire, where they will fall asleep, into the deepest of sleeps, with a dream hoop over the mantel, until the

fire dwindles and Jim must get up and take the balloon gloves off
and go outside and get another log for the fire.

Jim's a tough man, a little on the short side, but heavy, about
170, 175 pounds. Still, I wouldn't like to be on his end of it when
Patsy gets crazy (though I can hardly imagine it, I have to go by
what Jim tells me), because she's taller than he is, has pretty good
reach, and is in such good shape. I have to say that Jim isn't.

I've been skiing with Patsy in December, when the snow is still
soft and fresh and the woods are silent, and we're looking for
feathers for her wreaths; and I can tell she has to hold back to keep
from leaving me behind without even thinking about it. She's the
best damn skier in the valley, and sometimes when I look out my
breakfast room window, even if there is a heavy snow falling, I'll
see her go trucking by, with a determined, wild, happy look on
her face, and a Walkman strapped to her hip: lifting those skis
and leaning forward and digging in with the poles, just flat-out
racing, jamming to her old sixties and seventies rock and roll;
escaping the winter, escaping her love for Jim, escaping everything.

*J*im and I hunt in the fall, waiting for the snows to come down
so he can run his trapline. He traps anything, everything—mink,
beaver, badger, coyote, wolf, panther, bear; but in the fall, what
we hunt is deer and grouse.

We don't go after the elk any more, which are still up so high,
and too hard to get to. Jim says he has a bad ticker, and perhaps
he does, because he stops and rests often, even deer hunting,
down in the low woods, along the creeks. We do a lot of still
hunting, where we sit camouflaged, waiting on a ridge for something to walk past below.

Jim doesn't own a horse; he's through with them, says he has
gotten them out of his system. He runs his traplines on a snowmo-

bile, of all things, loud and obnoxious in the winter stillness, but he says it's faster (though not as dependable: it can't tell where the ice is too thin, beneath the snow, the way a horse can; he's ditched several into frozen streams that way, has barely gotten out alive, miles from home and twenty below, with dark coming on, sopping wet). Galena Jim is the last tough man there is, for a fact—but it's because he's still got that boy in him, some part he flat-out refuses to let go of. . . . And so in the fall, when we shoot our deer, I am the one who has to pack it out, because of Jim's bad ticker and because he does not own a horse. He delights in shooting the biggest deer in the most remote places, places so far from a road that a helicopter with a winch-cable couldn't get the deer out. And sometimes, for two or three days, we'll pack the deer out, me pulling a travois-sled we've lashed together, dragging the cleaned deer out, Galena Jim walking beside me, or behind, whistling, smoking his pipe; *sauntering*, with his rifle strapped to his back, carrying a walking stick: out for a stroll.

I'll be lunging up the hills—leaping forward in the harness we've fashioned for me, trying to get old Jim's big deer out of the woods; and he'll do his sharpshooting trick of knocking the heads off grouse as we come upon them on the trail, leaving them headless, spinning in the pine needles, fresh juicy meat for supper. And that's how we'll go through the woods, moving back down out of Canada, where the deer are larger and where there are no other hunters, and no roads—a hell of a good place to get lost— and we'll finally work our way back to the one thin road that goes up above the Moyie River, the one with the gate.

We'll load up, and turn around at the end of the road (about ten miles into Canada) and drive back out, locking the gate behind us. Another trophy deer for Galena Jim Ontz. Sometimes I get one too, though as I get older, I would rather pull only one deer, instead of two.

One year, when I was twenty-five—my strongest year—we got

a moose as well as two deer. But now when we come across a moose in the woods, I shout and whistle and throw rocks at it, before Jim can shoot. Even at twenty-five, it took me a week to get the moose (and two deer) out of there.

But we did get them out.

"Man, you're okay," Galena Jim says at the end of each sled-pulling day. He's a good cook, the best: those grouse on sticks, and potatoes in the coals; gravy from the deer meat, poured over the potatoes, and mashed. Jim knows all the names of the stars and constellations, and the *precise* distance we are from each of them (unless he is making it up, which I do not think he is). He points out the stars, so many of them, with a branch, and tells me the distance, in light years, as if he's been judging that particular star for a long time, wondering if he could somehow get there. He likes the trapping season best, and that's when he goes out alone, when everyone else (except Patsy) is trapped by the snow.

We'll sit there, so high in the Canadian Rockies, and watch clouds pass over the moon, feel the bite of what feels like the edges of eternity, a certain forever-aspect to things, as if this is the way it should always be up in this country—frigid, locked-in and cold, with springtime and yellow-flowered summer only an accident, which will, one of these years, not even bother happening. . . .

When we hunt, Galena Jim drinks whiskey in the evenings, telling me about those stars, and he tells me other things, things that no one else knows, maybe not even Patsy. Jim has a son, Buck, nineteen years old, who is in the state prison in Choteau, a lifer, maximum security, for killing a man. Buck is his son from a long-ago marriage, his only son. Buck's closer to my age than I am to Jim's. I don't know if Patsy knows about it or not. Somehow, I don't think she does. Jim doesn't talk about it much. Usually he just talks around the edges, like: "Wonder what Ol' Buck's doing tonight?" or something like that.

Or he'll talk about what it was like when he was nineteen, and twenty—things he used to do, and all the things he's done since. He'll ask me some of the things I've done, some of the things I've seen.

Not much, I'll feel like telling him, because it *doesn't* feel like much, not yet. That's part of the reason I hang around with Jim Ontz. But I can't tell him that. I know it'll let him down.

So instead I'll tell him about brown trout I've caught in Idaho, doubling their size, and the amount of time it took to land them. I'll make up lies about beautiful women I've loved, married women, women who've done these unbelievable things, and it's what we're supposed to talk about, out there in the woods like that, and it seems to make Galena Jim feel both happy and sad—better, in a way—and he laughs, looks over at me and laughs, and I think it even makes him able to get to sleep.

Hunting in a land where no one else can get to; bringing deer out of deep canyons and gorges that no one else could get them out of. I've still got my legs, my lower back: those Octobers, those early Novembers, we can do anything. Galena Jim said once that he had been thinking about breaking his son out of jail, but that was the only time he said that to me, never again, and I didn't know what to say. I didn't know if I'd let him down by not volunteering, or what. I don't know what I'd do if he brought it up again, and asked me to help.

I think that I would have to help him.

What I believe is this: that when Jim was young, he spent a lot of time on the circuit, trying to make it big, and not enough time around the house. I think that he has had his fill of horses, that maybe he has made some kind of promise to himself about never getting on them again.

I think maybe too that in winter, when everyone else is trapped, bound by their cabins, he gets so far out into the woods, in such a blowing wind, that he forgets where he is, even who he is.

I think he imagines he is his son, twenty years old, running the snowmobile along the frozen river, then stopping and getting off and walking up to his deadfall or his line-set: pulling the chain up out of the frozen waters, his eyes tearing and blurring in the cold—lifting the chain up, out there so far away from anyone, where no one can see, to find out if his luck has changed from yesterday, and what lies ahead in the next trap, and the next, and the next.

I have seen Galena Jim ride a moose before. Not showing off for anyone, unless it was just me—I was the only one with him. We were driving up the part of Hellroaring Road where the old World War II asphalt ends from the logging days and it goes to weeds and dirt—up above Pete Creek Road, up above everything, almost into Canada—and it was near the pass, where you go over from Montana into Idaho. Jim was driving, we were looking for grouse, and we came upon this big bull moose standing in the middle of the road. He was taller than the truck: the largest I'd ever seen, with a spread of palm-antlers as wide as a breakfast table.

Jim had been talking about food, about his favorite recipes for grouse, and for trout, and everything—he was supposed to go into Libby and cook dinner for Tiger, and was planning the menu, deciding what kind of wine to have with the meal—and this moose was suddenly in front of us, looking like he wanted to charge us, but turning instead, and running down the road ahead of us, like a blocker, clearing a path for us across the state line or something—and the moose wouldn't jump off the road, wouldn't veer to either side. Jim was gunning the truck, we were going thirty-five, almost forty miles an hour, right behind him—and Jim told me to take the wheel and the gas pedal, and climbed out onto the roof before I could say anything.

No one was around to see any of this. I couldn't understand why he was doing it.

He gave me the thumbs-up signal, and we pulled even with the big moose, racing alongside him, forty miles an hour with his clumsy, hoof-floating gallop, and he looked fierce, angry, out-raged; and that was before Jim leaped on his back, like something falling from the sky.

He clung to the big moose like a midget. The moose veered off the road and plowed through a bunch of low alder and fir, knocking Jim off, and then, like a bad bull in the rodeo, the moose came back up the hill, trying to gore Jim, to trample him; and I got the .30–.30 out, and was firing it into the air, and honking the horn, but couldn't shoot the moose, because Jim was in the way, running and scrambling, diving around rocks and rolling under logs, clutching his heart.

The moose lost Jim then, somehow, and came after the truck, and I was free to shoot it then; but I did not want to shoot a moose out of season, and especially such a fine moose as this one, and I did not know what Jim wanted me to do—what he would have done—and so I did not fire, and the moose slammed into the side of the truck and shook it, rocked it on its springs, roaring and coughing like a bull, and then it ran back down into the woods and disappeared.

I gave Jim some water and held his head up, propped him against a rock. The left side of his face was drawn down and twitching slightly. He didn't have any color, and for a moment, broken and hurt like that, almost helpless, he seemed like my friend rather than a teacher of any sort; and he seemed young, too, like he could have been just anybody, instead of Galena Jim Ontz, who had been thrown by a moose; and we sat there all afternoon, he with his eyes closed, resting, saving up, breathing slowly with cracked ribs.

It was only late summer and did not get dark until around ten o'clock. By the time Jim finally felt strong enough for me to help him into the truck, a low full moon had come up, and I did not know how to make the ride down the Hellroaring Road any less rough, but I went as slow as I could, and looked over to see how he was taking it.

He didn't look to be in pain so much as just sick feeling, as if he had done something wrong, had made a mistake somewhere.

"You're a good boy," he grunted when we finally got down off the road and back into the valley. I knew that in Libby, Tiger would be cursing him, maybe throwing things because he had not shown up; and I knew too that when we pulled up the driveway, with his truck battered and me getting out first, that Patsy would be frightened, that it would be like the worst of the dreams she never had; fearing the worst, knowing about his heart, and knowing about Jim. We drove with the windows down and a cool breeze in our faces, all the pastures bathed in bright silver moonlight, and the mountains all around the valley like a wall, holding us in.

The road sparkled and glittered in front of us, a path of where Jim had once been; a road one might encounter only in a dream. It was a road he had helped make, and we flew across it, rushing to get home.

THE WATCH

~⌒~

When Hollingsworth's father, Buzbee, was seventy-seven years old, he was worth a thousand dollars, that summer and fall. His name was up in all the restaurants and convenience stores, all along the interstate, and the indistinctions on the dark photocopies taped to doors and walls made him look distinguished, like someone else. The Xerox sheets didn't even say *Reward, Lost,* or *Missing.* They just got right to the point: *Mr. Buzbee, $1,000.*

The country Buzbee had disappeared in was piney woods, in the center of the state, away from the towns, the Mississippi—away from everything. There were swamps and ridges, and it was the hottest part of the state, and hardly anyone lived there. If they did, it was on those ridges, not down in the bottoms, and there were sometimes fields that had been cleared by hand, though the soil was poor and red, and could really grow nothing but tall lime-colored grass that bent in the wind like waves in a storm, and was good for horses, and nothing else—no crops, no cattle, nothing worth a damn—and Hollingsworth did not doubt that Buzbee, who had just recently taken to pissing in his pants, was alive, perhaps even lying down in the deep grass somewhere, to be spiteful, like a dog.

Hollingsworth knew the reward he was offering wasn't much.

He had a lot more money than that, but he read the papers and he knew that people in Jackson, the big town seventy miles north, offered that much every week, when their dogs ran off, or their cats went away somewhere to have kittens. Hollingsworth had offered only $1,000 for his father because $900 or some lesser figure would have seemed cheap—and some greater number would have made people think he was sad and missed the old man. It really cracked Hollingsworth up, reading about those lawyers in Jackson who would offer $1,000 for their tramp cats. He wondered how they came upon those figures—if they knew what a thing was really worth when they liked it.

It was lonely without Buzbee—it was bad, it was much too quiet, especially in the evenings—and it was the first time in his life that Hollingsworth had ever heard such a silence. Sometimes cyclists would ride past his dried-out barn and country store, and there was one who would sometimes stop for a Coke, sweaty, breathing hard, and he was more like some sort of draft animal than a person, so intent was he upon his speed, and he never had time to chat with Hollingsworth, to spin tales. He said his name was Jesse; he would say hello, gulp his Coke, and then this Jesse would be off, hurrying to catch up with the others.

Hollingsworth tried to guess the names of the other cyclists. He felt he had a secret over them: giving them names they didn't know they had. He felt as if he owned them, as if he had them on some invisible string and could pull them back in just by muttering their names. He called all the others by French names—François, Pierre, Jacques—as they all rode French bicycles with an unpronounceable name—and he thought they were pansies, delicate, for having been given such soft and fluttering names—but he liked Jesse, and even more, he liked Jesse's bike, which was a black Schwinn, a heavy old bike that Hollingsworth saw made Jesse struggle hard to stay up with the Frenchmen.

Hollingsworth watched them ride, like a pack of animals, up

and down the weedy, abandoned roads in the heat, disappearing into the shimmer that came up out of the road and the fields: the cyclists disappeared into the mirages, tracking a straight line, and then, later in the day—sitting on his porch, waiting—Hollingsworth would see them again when they came riding back out of the mirages.

*T*he very first time that Jesse had peeled off from the rest of the pack and stopped by Hollingsworth's ratty-ass grocery for a Coke—the sound the old bottle made, sliding down the chute, Hollingsworth still had the old formula Cokes, as no one—no one—ever came to his old leaning barn of a store, set back on the hill off the deserted road—that first time, Hollingsworth was so excited at having a visitor that he couldn't speak. He just kept swallowing, filling his stomach fuller and fuller with air—and the sound the old Coke bottle made sliding down the chute made Hollingsworth feel as if he had been struck in the head with it, as if he had been waiting at the bottom of the chute. No one had been out to his place since his father ran away: just the sheriff, once.

The road past Hollingsworth's store was the road of a ghost town. There had once been a good community, a big one—back at the turn of the century—down in the bottom, below his store—across the road, across the wide fields—rich growing grasses there, from the river's flooding—the Bayou Pierre, which emptied into the Mississippi—and down in the tall hardwoods, with trees so thick that three men, holding arms, could not circle them, there had been a colony, a fair-sized town actually, that shipped cotton down the bayou in the fall, when the waters started to rise again.

The town had been called Hollingsworth.

But in 1903 the last survivors had died of yellow fever, as had happened in almost every other town in the state—strangely enough, those lying closest to swamps and bayous, where yellow fever had always been a problem, were the last towns to go under, the most resistant—and then in the years that followed, the new towns that re-established themselves in the state did not choose to locate near Hollingsworth again. Buzbee's father had been one of the few who left before the town died, though he had contracted it, the yellow fever, and both Buzbee's parents died shortly after Buzbee was born.

Malaria came again in the 1930s, and got Buzbee's wife—Hollingsworth's mother—when Hollingsworth was born, but Buzbee and his new son stayed, dug in and refused to leave the store. When Hollingsworth was fifteen, they both caught it again, but fought it down, together, as it was the kind that attacked only every other day—a different strain than before—and their days of fever alternated, so that they were able to take care of each other: cleaning up the spitting and the vomiting of black blood; covering each other with blankets when the chills started, and building fires in the fireplace, even in summer. And they tried all the roots in the area, all the plants, and somehow—for they did not keep track of what they ate, they only sampled everything, anything that grew—pine boughs, cattails, wild carrots—they escaped being buried. Cemeteries were scattered throughout the woods and fields; nearly every place that was high and windy had one.

So the fact that no one ever came to their store, that there never had been any business, was nothing for Buzbee and Hollingsworth; everything would always be a secondary calamity, after the two years of yellow fever, and burying everyone, everything. Waking up in the night, with a mosquito biting them, and wondering if it had the fever. There were cans of milk on the shelves in their store that were forty years old; bags of potato chips that were twenty years old, because neither of them liked potato chips.

*H*ollingsworth would sit on his heels on the steps and tremble whenever Jesse and the others rode past, and on the times when Jesse turned in and came up to the store, so great was Hollingsworth's hurry to light his cigarette and then talk, slowly, the way it was supposed to be done in the country, the way he had seen it in his imagination, when he thought about how he would like his life to really be—that he spilled two cigarettes, and had barely gotten the third lit and drawn one puff when Jesse finished his Coke and then stood back up, and put the wet empty bottle back in the wire rack, waved, and rode off, the great backs of his calves and hamstrings working up and down in swallowing shapes, like things trapped in a sack. So Hollingsworth had to wait again for Jesse to come back, and by the next time, he had decided for certain that Buzbee was just being spiteful.

*B*efore Buzbee had run away, sometimes Hollingsworth and Buzbee had cooked their dinners in the evenings, and other times they had driven into a town and ordered something, and looked around at people, and talked to the waitresses—but now, in the evenings, Hollingsworth stayed around, so as not to miss Jesse should he come by, and he ate briefly, sparingly, from his stocks on the shelves: dusty cans of Vienna sausage; sardines, and rock crackers. Warm beer, brands that had gone out of business a decade earlier, two decades. Holding out against time was difficult, but was also nothing after holding out against death. In cheating death, Hollingsworth and Buzbee had continued to live, had survived, but also, curiously, they had lost an edge of some sort: nothing would ever be quite as intense, nothing would ever really matter, after the biggest struggle.

The old cans of food didn't have any taste, but Hollingsworth didn't mind. He didn't see that it mattered much. Jesse said the other bikers wouldn't stop because they thought the Cokes were bad for them: cut their wind, slowed them down.

Hollingsworth had to fight down the feelings of wildness sometimes, now that his father was gone. Hollingsworth had never married, never had a friend other than his father. He had everything brought to him by the grocery truck, on the rarest of orders, and by the mail. He subscribed to *The Wall Street Journal.* It was eight days late by the time he received it—but he read it—and before Buzbee had run away they used to tell each other stories. They would start at sundown and talk until ten o'clock: Buzbee relating the ancient things, and Hollingsworth telling about everything that was in the paper. Buzbee's stories were always better. They were things that had happened two, three miles away.

As heirs to the town, Hollingsworth and Buzbee had once owned, back in the thirties, over two thousand acres of land—cypress and water oak, down in the swamp, and great thick bull pines, on the ridges—but they'd sold almost all of it to the timber companies—a forty- or eighty-acre tract every few years—and now they had almost no land left, just the shack in which they lived.

But they had bushels and bushels of money, kept in peach bushel baskets in their closet, stacked high. They didn't miss the land they had sold, but wished they had more, so that the pulpwood cutters would return: they had enjoyed the sound of the chain saws.

Back when they'd been selling their land, and having it cut, they would sit on their porch in the evenings and listen to it, the far-off cutting, as if it were music: picturing the great trees falling; and feeling satisfied, somehow, each time they heard one hit.

*T*he first thing Jesse did in the mornings when he woke up was to check the sky, and then, stepping out onto the back porch, naked, the wind. If there wasn't any, he would be relaxed and happy with his life. If it was windy—even the faintest stir against his shaved ankles, up and over his round legs—he would scowl, a grimace of concentration, and go in and fix his coffee. There couldn't be any letting up on windy days, and if there was a breeze in the morning, it would build to true and hard wind for sure by afternoon: the heat of the fields rising, cooling, falling back down: blocks of air as slippery as his biking suit, sliding all up and down the roads, twisting through trees, looking for places to blow, paths of least resistance.

*T*here was so much Hollingsworth wanted to tell someone! Jesse, or even François, Jacques, Pierre! Buzbee was gone! He and Buzbee had told each other all the old stories, again and again. There wasn't anything new, not really, not of worth, and hadn't been for a long time. Hollingsworth had even had to resort to fabricating things, pretending he was reading them in the paper, to match Buzbee during the last few years of storytelling. And now, alone, his imagination was turning in on itself, and growing, like the most uncontrollable kind of cancer, with nowhere to go, and in the evenings he went out on the porch and looked across the empty highway, into the waving fields in the ebbing winds, and beyond, down to the blue line of trees along the bayou, where he knew Buzbee was hiding out, and Hollingsworth would ring the dinner bell, loudly and clearly, with a grim anger, and he would hope, scanning the fields, that Buzbee would stand up and wave, and come back in.

*J*esse came by for another Coke in the second week of July. There was such heat. Hollingsworth had called in to Crystal Springs and had the asphalt truck come out and grade and level his gravel, pour hot slick new tar down over it, and smooth it out: it cooled, slowly, and was beautiful, almost iridescent, like a black-snake in the bright green grass: it glowed its way across the yard as if it were made of glass, a path straight to the store, coming in off the road. It beckoned.

"So you got a new driveway," Jesse said, looking down at his feet.

The bottle was already in his hand; he was already taking the first sip.

Nothing lasted; nothing!

Hollingsworth clawed at his chest, his shirt pocket, for cigarettes. He pulled them out and got one and lit it, and then sat down and said, slowly, "Yes." He looked out at the fields and couldn't remember a single damn story.

He groped, and faltered.

"You may have noticed there's a sudden abundance of old coins, especially quarters, say, 1964, 1965, the ones that have still got some silver in them," Hollingsworth said casually, but it wasn't the story in his heart.

"This is nice," Jesse said. "This is like what I race on sometimes." The little tar strip leading in to the Coke machine and Hollingsworth's porch was as black as a snake that had just freshly shed its skin, and was as smooth and new. Hollingsworth had been sweeping it twice a day, to keep twigs off it, and waiting.

It was soft and comfortable to stand on; Jesse was testing it with his foot—pressing down on it, pleasurably, admiring the surface and firmness, yet also the give of it.

"The Russians hoarded them, is my theory, got millions of them from our mints in the sixties, during the cold war," Hollingsworth said quickly. Jesse was halfway through with his Coke. This wasn't the way it was with Buzbee at all. "They've since subjected them to radiation—planted them amongst our populace."

Jesse's calves looked like whales going away; his legs, like things from another world. They were grotesque when they moved and pumped.

"I saw a man who looked like you," Jesse told Hollingsworth in August.

Jesse's legs and deep chest were taking on a hardness and slickness that hadn't been there before. He was drinking only half his Coke, and then slowly pouring the rest of it on the ground, while Hollingsworth watched, crestfallen: the visit already over, cut in half by dieting, and the mania for speed and distance.

"Except he was real old," Jesse said. "I think he was the man they're looking for." Jesse didn't know Hollingsworth's first or last name; he had never stopped to consider it.

Hollingsworth couldn't speak. The Coke had made a puddle and was fizzing, popping quietly in the dry grass. The sun was big and orange across the fields, going down behind the blue trees. It was beginning to cool. Doves were flying past, far over their heads, fat from the fields and late-summer grain. Hollingsworth wondered what Buzbee was eating, where he was living, why he had run away.

"He was fixing to cross the road," said Jesse.

He was standing up: balancing carefully, in the little cleat shoes that would skid out from underneath him from time to time when he tried to walk in them. He didn't use a stopwatch the way other cyclists did, but he knew he was getting faster, because just recently he had gotten the quiet, almost silent sensation—just a soft hushing—of falling, the one that athletes, and sometimes other people, get when they push deeper and deeper into their sport, until—like pushing through one final restraining layer of tissue, the last and thinnest, easiest one—they are falling, slowly, and there is nothing left in their life to stop them, no work is necessary, things are just happening, and they suddenly have all the time in the world to perfect their sport, because that's all there is, one day, finally.

"I tried to lay the bike down and get off and chase him," Jesse said. "But my legs cramped up."

He put the Coke bottle in the rack.

The sun was in Hollingsworth's eyes: it was as if he were being struck blind. He could smell only Jesse's heavy body odor, and could feel only the heat still radiating from his legs, like thick andirons taken from a fire: legs like a horse's, standing there, with veins wrapping them, spidery, beneath the thin browned skin.

"He was wearing dirty old overalls and no shirt," said Jesse. "And listen to this. He had a live carp tucked under one arm, and it didn't have a tail left on it. I had the thought that he had been eating on that fish's tail, chewing on it."

Jesse was giving a speech. Hollingsworth felt himself twisting down and inside with pleasure, like he was swooning. Jesse kept talking, nailing home the facts.

"He turned and ran like a deer, back down through the field, down toward the creek, and into those trees, still holding on to the fish." Jesse turned and pointed. "I was thinking that if we could catch him on your tractor, run him down and lasso him, I'd split the reward money with you." Jesse looked down at his legs: the round swell of them so ballooned and great that they hid completely his view of the tiny shoes below him. "I could never catch him by myself, on foot, I don't think," he said, almost apologetically. "For an old fucker, he's fast. There's no telling what he thinks he's running from."

"Hogson, the farmer over on Green Gable Road, has got himself some hounds," Hollingsworth heard himself saying, in a whisper. "He bought them from the penitentiary, when they turned mean, for five hundred dollars. They can track anything. They'll run the old man to Florida if they catch his scent; they won't ever let up."

Hollingsworth was remembering the hounds: black and tan, the colors of late frozen night, and cold honey in the sun, in the morning, and he was picturing the dogs moving through the forest, with Jesse and himself behind them: camping out! The dogs straining on their heavy leashes! Buzbee, slightly ahead of them, on the run, leaping logs, crashing the undergrowth, splashing through the bends and loops in the bayou: savage swamp birds, rafts of them, darkening the air as they rose in their fright, leaping up in entire rookeries . . . cries in the forest, it would be like the jungle . . . . It might take days! Stories around the campfire! He would tear off a greasy leg of chicken, from the grill, reach across to hand it to Jesse, and tell him about anything, everything.

"We should try the tractor first," Jesse said, thinking ahead. It was hard to think about a thing other than bicycling, and he was frowning and felt awkward, exposed, and, also, trapped: cut off from the escape route. "But if he gets down into the woods, we'll probably have to use the dogs."

Hollingsworth was rolling up his pants leg, cigarette still in hand, to show Jesse the scar from the hunting accident when he was twelve: his father had said he thought he was a deer, and had shot him. Buzbee had been twenty-six.

"I'm like you," Hollingsworth said faithfully. "I can't run

worth a damn, either." But Jesse had already mounted his bike:
he was moving away, down the thin black strip, like a pilot taking
a plane down a runway, to lift off, or like a fish running to sea;
he entered the dead highway, which had patches of weeds growing up even in its center, and he stood up in the clips and
accelerated away, down through the trees, with the wind at his
back, going home.

He was gone almost immediately.

Hollingsworth did not want to go back inside. The store had
turned dark; the sun was down behind the trees. Hollingsworth
sat down on the porch and watched the empty road. His mother
had died giving birth to him. She, like his father, had been
fourteen. He and his father had always been more like brothers
to each other than anything else. Hollingsworth could remember
playing a game with his father, perhaps when he was seven or
eight, and his father then would have been twenty-one or so—
Jesse's age, roughly—and his father would run out into the field
and hide, on their old homestead—racing down the hill, arms
windmilling, and disappearing suddenly, diving down into the tall
grass, while Hollingsworth—Quirter, Quirt—tried to find him.
They played that game again and again, more than any other
game in the world, and at all times of the year, not just in the
summer.

*B*uzbee had a favorite tree, and he sat up in the low branch
of it often and looked back in the direction from which he had
come. He saw the bikers every day. There weren't ever cars on
the road. The cyclists sometimes picnicked at a little roadside
table, oranges and bottles of warm water and candy bars by the
dozens—he had snuck out there in the evenings, before, right at
dusk, and sorted through their garbage, nibbled some of the

orange peelings—and he was nervous, in his tree, whenever they stopped for any reason.

Buzbee had not in the least considered going back to his maddened son. He shifted on the branch and watched the cyclists eat their oranges. His back was slick with sweat, and he was rank, like the worst of animals. He and all the women bathed in the evenings in the bayou, in the shallows, rolling around in the mud. The women wouldn't go out any deeper. Snakes swam in evil S-shapes, back and forth, as if patrolling. He was starting to learn the women well, and many of them were like his son in every regard, in that they always wanted to talk, it seemed—this compulsion to communicate, as if it could be used to keep something else away, something big and threatening. He thought about what the cold weather would be like, November and beyond, himself trapped, as it were, in the abandoned palmetto shack, with all of them around the fireplace, talking, for four months.

He slid down from the tree and started out into the field, toward the cyclists—the women watched him go—and in the heat, in the long walk across the field, he became dizzy, started to fall several times, and for the briefest fragments of time he kept forgetting where he was, imagined that one of the cyclists was his son, that he was coming back in from the game that they used to play, and he stopped, knelt down in the grass and pretended to hide. Eventually, though, the cyclists finished eating, got up and rode away, down the road again. Buzbee watched them go, then stood up and turned and raced back down into the woods, to the women. He had become very frightened, for no reason, out in the field like that.

*B*uzbee had found the old settlement after wandering around in the woods for a week. There were carp in the bayou, and gar, and catfish, and he wrestled the large ones out of the shallow oxbows that had been cut off from the rest of the water. He caught alligators, too, the small ones.

He kept a small fire going, continuously, to keep the mosquitoes away, and as he caught more and more of the big fish, he hung them from the branches in his clearing, looped vine through their huge jaws and hung them like villains, all around in his small clearing, like the most ancient of burial grounds: all these vertical fish, out of the water, mouths gaping in silent death, as if preparing to ascend: they were all pointing up.

The new pleasure of being alone sometimes stirred Buzbee so that he ran from errand to errand. He was getting ready for this new life, and with fall and winter coming on, he felt young.

After a couple of weeks, he had followed the bayou upstream, toward town, backtracking the water's sluggishness; he slept under the large logs that had fallen across it like netting, and he swatted at the mosquitoes that swarmed him whenever he stopped moving, in the evenings, and he had kept going, even at night. The moon came down through the bare limbs of the swamp-rotted ghost trees, skeleton-white, disease-killed, but as he got higher above the swamp and closer to the town, near daylight, the water moved faster, had some circulation, was still alive, and the mosquitoes were not a threat.

He lay under a boxcar on the railroad tracks and looked across the road at the tired women going in and out of the washateria: moving so slowly, as if old. They were in their twenties, their thirties, their forties: they carried their baskets of wet clothes in front of them with a bumping, side-to-side motion, as if they were going to quit living on the very next step; their forearms sweated, glistened, and the sandals on their wide feet made flopping sounds, and he wanted to tell them about his settlement. He wanted five or six, ten or twenty of them. He wanted them walking around barefooted on the dark earth beneath his trees, beneath his hanging catfish and alligators, by the water, in the swamp.

He stole four chickens and a rooster that night, hooded their eyes, and put them in a burlap sack, put three eggs in each of his shirt pockets, too, after sucking ten of them dry, greedily, gulping, in the almost wet brilliance of the moon, behind a chicken farm back west of town, along the bayou—and then he continued on down its banks, the burlap sack thrown over his back, the chickens and rooster warm against his damp body, and calm, waiting.

He stopped when he came out of the green and thick woods, over a little ridge, and looked down into the country where the bayous slowed to heavy swamp and where the white and dead trees were and the bad mosquitoes lived—and he sat down and leaned his old back against a tree, and watched the moon and its blue light shining on the swamp, with his chickens. He waited until the sun came up and it got hot, and the mosquitoes had gone away, before starting down toward the last part of his journey, back to his camp.

The rest of the day he gathered seeds and grain from the little raised hummocks and grassy spots in the woods, openings in the forest, to use for feed for the chickens, which moved in small crooked shapes of white, like little ghosts in the woods, all through his camp, but they did not leave it. The rooster flew up into a low tree and stared wildly, golden-eyed, down into the bayou. For weeks Buzbee had been hunting the quinine bushes said to have been planted there during the big epidemic, and on that day he found them, because the chickens went straight to them and began pecking at them as Buzbee had never seen chickens peck: they flew up into the leaves, smothered their bodies against the bushes as if mating with them, so wild were they to get to the berries.

Buzbee's father had planted the bushes, had received the seeds from South America, on a freighter that he met in New Orleans the third year of the epidemic, and he had returned with them to the settlement, that third year, when everyone went down finally.

The plants had not done well; they kept rotting, and never, in Buzbee's father's time, bore fruit or made berries. Buzbee had listened to his father tell the story about how they rotted—but also how, briefly, they had lived, even flourished, for a week or two, and how the settlement had celebrated and danced, and cooked alligators and cattle, and prayed: and everyone in the settlement had planted quinine seeds, all over the woods, for miles, in every conceivable location . . . and Buzbee knew immediately, when the chickens began to cluck and feed, that it was the quinine berries, which they knew instinctively they must eat, and he went and gathered all the berries, and finally, he knew, he was safe.

The smoke from his fire, down in the low bottom, had spread through the swamp, and from above would have looked as if that portion of the bayou, going into the tangled dead trees, had simply disappeared: a large spill of white, a fuzzy, milky spot—and then, on the other side of the spill, coming out again, bayou once more.

Buzbee was relieved to have the berries, and he let the fire go down: he let it die. He sat against his favorite tree by the water and watched for small alligators. When he saw one, he would leap into the water, splash and swim across to meet it, and wrestle it out of the shallows and into the mud, where he would kill it savagely.

But the days were long, and he did not see that many alligators, and many of the ones he did see were a little too large, sometimes far too large. Still, he had almost enough for winter, as it stood:

those hanging from the trees, along with the gaping catfish, spun slowly in the breeze of fall coming, and if he waited and watched, eventually he would see one. He sat against the tree and watched, and ate berries, chewed them slowly, pleasuring in their sour taste.

He imagined that they soured his blood: that they made him taste bad to the mosquitoes, and kept them away. Though he noticed they were still biting him, more even, now that the smoke was gone. But he got used to it.

A chicken had disappeared, probably to a snake, but also possibly to anything, anything.

The berries would keep him safe.

He watched the water. Sometimes there would be the tiniest string of bubbles rising, from where an alligator was stirring in the mud below.

*T*wo of the women from the laundry came out of the woods, tentatively, having left their homes, following the bayou, to see if it was true: what they had heard. It was dusk, and their clothes were torn and their faces wild. Buzbee looked up and could see the fear, and he wanted to comfort them. He did not ask what had happened at their homes, what fear could make the woods and the bayou journey seem less frightening. They stayed back in the trees, frozen, and would not come with him, even when he took each by the hand, until he saw what it was that was horrifying them: the grinning reptiles, the dried fish, spinning from the trees—and he explained to them that he had put them there to smoke, for food, for the winter.

"They smell good," said the shorter one, heavier than her friend, her skin a deep black, like some poisonous berry. Her face was shiny.

Her friend slapped at a mosquito.

"Here," said Buzbee, handing them some berries. "Eat these."

But they made faces and spat them out when they tasted the bitterness.

Buzbee frowned. "You'll get sick if you don't eat them," he said. "You won't make it otherwise."

They walked past him, over to the alligators, and reached out to the horned, hard skin, and touched them fearfully, ready to run, making sure the alligators were truly harmless.

"*D*on't you ever, you know, get lonely for girls?" Hollingsworth asked, like a child. It was only four days later: but Jesse was back for another half-Coke. The other bikers had ridden past almost an hour earlier: a fast rip-rip-rip, and then, much later, Jesse had come up the hill, pedaling hard, but moving slower.

He was trying, but he couldn't stay up with them. He had thrown his bike down angrily, and glowered at Hollingsworth, when he stalked up to the Coke machine, scowled at him as if it was Hollingsworth's fault.

"I got a whore," Jesse said, looking behind him and out across the road. The pasture was green and wet, and fog, like mist, hung over it, steaming from a rain earlier in the day. Jesse was lying; he didn't have anyone, hadn't had anyone in over a year—everybody knew he was slow in his group, and they shunned him for that—and Jesse felt as if he was getting farther and farther away from ever wanting anyone, or anything. He felt like everything was a blur: such was the speed at which he imagined he was trying to travel. Beyond the fog in the pasture were the trees, clear and dark and washed from the rain, and smelling good, even at this distance. Hollingsworth wished he had a whore. He wondered if Jesse would let him use his. He wondered if maybe she would be available if Jesse was to get fast and go off to the Olympics, or something.

"What does she cost?" Hollingsworth asked timidly.

Jesse looked at him in disgust. "I didn't mean it *that* way," he said. He looked tired, as if he was holding back, just a few seconds, from having to go back out on the road. Hollingsworth leaned closer, eagerly, sensing weakness, tasting hesitation. His senses were sharp from deprivation: he could tell, even before Jesse could, that Jesse was feeling thick, laggard, dulled. He knew Jesse was going to quit. He knew it the way a farmer might see that rain was coming.

"I mean," sighed Jesse, "that I got an old lady. A woman friend. A girl."

"What's her name?" Hollingsworth said quickly. He would make Jesse so tired that he would never ride again. They would sit around on the porch and talk forever, all of the days.

"Jemima."

Hollingsworth wanted her, just for her name.

"That's nice," he said, in a smaller voice.

It seemed to Hollingsworth that Jesse was getting his energy back. But he had felt the tiredness, and maybe, Hollingsworth hoped, it would come back.

"I found out the old man is your father," said Jesse. He was looking out at the road. He still wasn't making any move toward it. Hollingsworth realized, as if he had been tricked, that perhaps Jesse was just waiting for the roads to dry up a little, to finish steaming.

"Yes," said Hollingsworth, "he has run away."

They looked at the fields together.

"He is not right," Hollingsworth said.

"The black women in town, the ones that do everyone's wash at the laundromat, say he is living down in the old yellow-fever community," Jesse said. "They say he means to stay, and that some of them have thought about going down there with him: the ones with bad husbands and too much work. He's been sneaking around the laundry late in the evenings, and promising them he'll cook for them, if any of them want to move down there with him. He says there aren't any snakes. They're scared the fever will come back, but he promises there aren't any snakes, that he killed them all, and a lot of them are considering it." Jesse related all this in a monotone, still watching the road, as if waiting for energy. The sun was burning the steam off. Hollingsworth felt damp, weak, unsteady, as if his mind was sweating with condensation from the knowledge, the way glasses suddenly fog up when you are walking into a humid setting.

"Sounds like he's getting lonely," Jesse said.

The steam was almost gone.

"He'll freeze this winter," Hollingsworth said, hopefully.

Jesse shook his head. "Sounds like he's got a plan. I suspect he'll have those women cutting firewood for him; fanning him with leaves; fishing, running traps, bearing children. Washing clothes."

"We'll catch him," Hollingsworth said, making a fist and smacking it in his palm. "And anyway, those women won't go down into those woods. Those woods are dark, and the yellow fever's still down there: I'll go into town, and tell them it is. I'll tell them Buzbee's spitting up black blood and shivering, and is crazy. Those women won't go down into those woods."

Jesse shook his head. He put the bottle into the rack. The road was dry; it looked clean, scrubbed, by the quick thunderstorm. "A lot of those women have got bruises on their arms, their faces, have got teeth missing, and their lives are too hard and without hope," Jesse said slowly, as if just for the first time seeing it. "Myself, I think they'll go down there in great numbers. I don't think yellow fever means anything compared to what they have, or will have." He turned to Hollingsworth and slipped a leg over his bike, got on, put his feet in the clips, steadied himself against the porch railing. "I bet by June next year you're going to have about twenty half brothers and half sisters."

When Jesse rode off, thickly, as if the simple heat of the air were a thing holding him back, there was no question, Hollingsworth realized, Jesse was exhausted, and fall was coming. Jesse was getting tired. He, Hollingsworth, and Buzbee, and the colored women at the washhouse, and other people would get tired, too. The temperatures would be getting cooler, milder, in a month or so, and the bikers would be riding harder than ever. There would be the smoke from fires, hunters down on the river, and at night the stars would be brighter, and people's sleep would be heavier, and deeper. Hollingsworth wondered just how fast those bikers wanted to go. Surely, he thought, they were already going fast enough. He didn't understand them. Surely, he thought, they didn't know what they were doing.

*T*he speeds that the end of June and the beginning of July brought, Jesse had never felt before, and he didn't trust them to last, didn't know if they could: and he tried to stay with the other riders, but didn't know if there was anything he could do to make the little speed he had last, in the curves, and that feeling, pounding up the hills; his heart working strong and smooth, like the wildest, easiest, most volatile thing ever invented. He tried to stay with them.

Hollingsworth, the old faggot, was running out into the road some days, trying to flag him down, for some piece of bullshit, but there wasn't time, and he rode past, not even looking at him, only staring straight ahead.

The doves started to fly. The year was moving along. A newspaper reporter wandered down, to do a short piece on the still-missing Buzbee. It was rumored he was living in an abandoned, rotting shack, deep into the darkest, lowest heart of the swamp. It was said that he had started taking old colored women, maids and such, women from the laundromat, away from town; that they were going back down into the woods with him and living there, and that he had them in a corral, like a herd of wild horses. The reporter's story slipped farther from the truth. It was all very mysterious, all rumor, and the reward was increased to $1,200 by Hollingsworth, as the days grew shorter after the solstice, and lonelier.

Jesse stopped racing. He just didn't go out one day; and when the Frenchmen came by for him, he pretended not to be in. He slept late and began to eat vast quantities of oatmeal. Sometimes, around noon, he would stop eating and get on his bike and ride slowly up the road to Hollingsworth's—sometimes the other bikers would pass him, moving as ever at great speed, all of them, and they would jeer at him, shout yah-yah, and then they were quickly gone; and he willed them to wreck, shut his eyes and tried to make it happen—picturing the whole pack of them getting tangled up, falling over one another, the way they tended to do, riding so close together.

*T*he next week he allowed himself a whole Coca-Cola, with Hollingsworth, on the steps of the store's porch. The old man swooned, and had to steady himself against the porch railing when he saw it was his true love. It was a dry summer. They talked more about Buzbee.

"He's probably averse to being captured," Hollingsworth said. "He probably won't go easy."

Jesse looked at his shoes, watched them, as if thinking about where they were made.

"If you were to help me catch him, I would give you my half of it," Hollingsworth said generously. Jesse watched his shoes.

Hollingsworth got up and went in the store, and came back

out with a hank of calf-rope lariat, heavy, gold as a fable, and corded.

"I been practicing," he said. There was a sawhorse standing across the drive, up on two legs, like a man, with a hat on it, and a coat, and Hollingsworth said nothing else, but twirled the lariat over his head and then flung it at the sawhorse, a mean heavy whistle over their heads, and the loop settled over the sawhorse, and Hollingsworth stepped back quickly and tugged, cinched the loop shut. The sawhorse fell over, and Hollingsworth began dragging it across the gravel, reeling it in as fast as he could.

"I could lasso you off that road if I wanted," Hollingsworth said.

Jesse thought about how the money would be nice. He thought about how it was in a wreck, too, when he wasn't able to get his feet free of the clips and had to stay with the bike, and roll over with it, still wrapped up in it. It was just the way his sport was.

"I've got to be going," he told Hollingsworth. When he stood up, though, he had been still too long, and his blood stayed down in his legs, and he saw spots and almost fell.

"Easy now, hoss," Hollingsworth cautioned; watching him eagerly, eyes narrowed, hoping for an accident and no more riding.

*T*he moonlight came in through Hollingsworth's window, onto his bed, all night—it was silver. It made things look different: ghostly. Hollingsworth lay on his back, looking up at the ceiling.

We'll get him, he thought. We'll find his ass. But he couldn't sleep, and the sound of his heart, the movement of his blood pulsing, was the roar of an ocean, and it wasn't right. His father did not belong down in those woods. No one did. There was nothing down there that Hollingsworth could see but reptiles and danger.

The moon was so bright that it washed out all stars. Hollingsworth listened to the old house. There was a blister on the inside of his finger from practicing with the lariat, and he fingered it and looked at the ceiling.

"*L*et's go hunt that old dog," Hollingsworth said—it was the first thing he said, after Jesse had gotten his bottle out of the machine and opened it—and like a molester, a crooner, Hollingsworth seemed to be drifting toward Jesse without moving his feet: just leaning forward, swaying closer and closer, as if moving in to smell blossoms. His eyes were a believer's blue, and for a moment, Jesse had no idea what he was talking about and felt dizzy. He looked into Hollingsworth's eyes, such a pale wash of light, such a pale blue that he knew the eyes had never seen anything factual, nothing of substance—and he laughed, thinking of Hollingsworth trying to catch Buzbee, or anything, on his own.

"We can split the reward money," Hollingsworth said again. He was grinning, smiling wildly, trying as hard as he could to show all his teeth and yet keep them close together, uppers and lowers touching. He breathed through the cracks in them in a low, pulsing whistle: in and out. He had never in his life drunk anything but water, and his teeth were startlingly white; they were just whittled down, was all, and puny from aging and time. He closed his eyes, squeezed them shut slowly, as if trying to remember something simple, like speech, or balance, or even breathing. He was like a turtle sunning on a log.

Jesse couldn't believe he was speaking. "Give me all of it," Jesse heard himself say.

"All of it," Hollingsworth agreed, his eyes still shut, and then he opened them and handed the money to Jesse slowly, ceremoniously, like a child paying for something at a store counter for the first time.

Jesse unlaced his shoes, and folded the bills in half and slid them down into the soles, putting bills in both shoes. He unlaced the drawstring to his pants and slid some down into the black dampness of his racing silks: down in the crotch, and padding the buttocks, and in front, high on the flatness of his abdomen, like a girdle, directly below the cinching lace of the drawstring, which he then tied again, tighter than it had been before.

Then he got on the bike and rode home, slowly, not racing anymore, not at all; through the late-day heat that had built up, but with fall in the air, the leaves on the trees hanging differently. There was some stillness everywhere. He rode on.

When he got home he carried the bike inside, as was his custom, and then undressed, peeling his suit off, with the damp bills fluttering slowly to the old rug, unfolding when they landed, and it surprised him at first to see them falling away from him like that, all around him, for he had forgotten that they were down there as he rode.

*B*uzbee was like a field general. The women were tasting freedom, and seemed to be like circus strongmen, muscled with great strength suddenly from not being told what to do, from not being beaten or yelled at. They laughed and talked, and were kind to Buzbee. He sat up in the tree in his old khaki pants, and watched, and whenever it looked like his feeble son and the ex-biker might be coming, he leaped down from the tree, and like monkeys they scattered into the woods: back to another, deeper, temporary camp they had built.

They splashed across the river like wild things, but they were laughing, there was no fear, not like there would have been in animals.

They knew they could get away. They knew that as long as they ran fast, they would make it.

Buzbee grinned too, panting, his eyes bright, and he watched the women's breasts float and bounce, riding high as they charged across; ankle-deep, knee-deep, waist-deep; hurrying to get away from his mad, lonely son: running fast and shrieking, because they were all afraid of the alligators.

Buzbee had a knife in one hand and a sharpened stick in the other, and he almost wished there would be an attack, so that he could be a hero.

The second camp was about two miles down into the swamp. No one had ever been that far into it, not ever. The mosquitoes were worse, too. There wasn't any dry land, not even a patch, so they sat on the branches, and dangled their feet, and waited. Sometimes they saw black bears splashing after fish, and turtles. There were more snakes, too, deeper back, but the women were still bruised, and some of them fingered their bruises and scars as they watched the snakes, but no one went back.

They made up songs, with which they pretended to make the snakes go away.

It wasn't too bad.

They sat through the night listening to the cries of birds, and when the woods began to grow light again, so faintly at first that they doubted it was happening, they would ease down into the water and start back toward their dry camp.

Hollingsworth would be gone, chased away by the mosquitoes, by the emptiness, and they would feel righteous, as if they'd won something: a victory.

None of them had a watch. They never knew what time it was, what day even.

"Gone," said Hollingsworth.

He was out of breath, out of shape. His shoelaces were untied, and there were burrs in his socks. The camp was empty. Just chickens. And the godawful reptiles, twisting from the trees.

"Shit almighty," said Jesse. His legs were cramping and he was bent over, massaging them: he wasn't used to walking.

Hollingsworth poked around in the little grass-and-wood shacks. He was quivering and kept saying, alternately, "Gone" and "Damn."

Jesse had to sit down, the pain in his legs was so bad. He put his feet together like a bear in the zoo and held them there, and rocked, trying to stretch them back out. He was frightened of the alligators, and he felt helpless, in his cramps, knowing that Buzbee could come up from behind with a club and rap him on the head, like one of the chickens, and he, Jesse, wouldn't even be able to get up to stop him or run.

Buzbee was in control.

"Shit. Damn. Gone," said Hollingsworth. He was running a hand through his thinning hair. He kicked a few halfhearted times at the shacks, but they were kicks of sorrow, not rage yet, and did no damage.

"We could eat the chickens," Jesse suggested, from his sitting position. "We could cook them on his fire and leave the bones all over camp." Jesse still had his appetite from his riding days, and was getting fat fast. He was eating all the time since he had stopped riding.

Hollingsworth turned to him, slightly insulted. "They belong to my father," he said.

Jesse continued to rock, but thought: My God, what a madman.

He rubbed his legs and rocked. The pain was getting worse.

There was a breeze stirring. They could hear the leather and rope creaking, as some of the smaller alligators moved. There was a big alligator hanging from a beech tree, about ten feet off the ground, and as they watched it, the leather cord snapped, from the friction, and the dead weight of the alligator crashed to the ground.

"The mosquitoes are getting bad," said Jesse, rising: hobbled, bent over. "We'd better be going."

But Hollingsworth was already scrambling up through the brush, up toward the brightness of sky above the field. He could see the sky, the space, through the trees, and knew the field was out there. He was frantic to get out of the woods; there was a burning in his chest, in his throat, and he couldn't breathe.

Jesse helped him across the field and got him home. He offered to ride into Crystal Springs, thirty miles, and make a call for an ambulance, but Hollingsworth waved him away.

"Just stay with me a little while," he said. "I'll be okay."

But the thought was terrifying to Jesse—of being in the same room with Hollingsworth, contained, and listening to him talk, forever, all day and through the night, doubtless.

"I have to go," Jesse said, and hurried out the door.

He got on his bike and started slowly for home. His knees were bumping against his belly, such was the quickness of his becoming fat, but the relief of being away from Hollingsworth was so great that he didn't mind.

Part of him wanted to be as he had been, briefly: iron, and fast, racing with the fastest people in the world, it seemed—he couldn't remember anything about them, only the blaze and rip of their speed, the *whish-whish* cutting sound they made, as a pack, tucking and sailing down around corners—but also, he was so tired of that, and it felt good to be away from it, for just a little while.

He could always go back.

His legs were still strong. He could start again any time. The sport of it, the road, would have him back. The other bikers would have him back, they would be happy to see him.

He thought all these things as he trundled fatly up the minor hills, the gradual rises: coasting—with relief—on the down sides.

Shortly before he got to the gravel turnoff, the little tree-lined road that led to his house, the other bikers passed him, coming from out of the west, and they screamed and howled at him, passing, and jabbed their thumbs down at him, as if they were trying to unplug a drain or poke a hole in something; they shrieked, and then they were gone, so quickly.

He wanted to hide somewhere, he was so ashamed of what he had lost, but there was nowhere to hide, for in a way it was still in him: the memory of it.

Later, he dreamed of going down into the woods, of joining Buzbee and starting over, wrestling alligators; but he only dreamed it—and in the morning, when he woke up, he was still heavy and slow, grounded.

He went into the kitchen, and looked in the refrigerator, and began taking things out. Maybe, he thought, Hollingsworth would up the reward money.

*B*uzbee enjoyed cooking for the women. It was going to be an early fall, and dry; they got to where they hardly noticed the mosquitoes that were always whining around them—a tiny buzzing—and they had stopped wearing clothes long ago. Buzbee pulled down hickory branches and climbed up in trees, often— and he sat hunkered above the women, looking down, just watching them move around in their lives, naked and happy, talking. More had come down the bayou since the first two, and they were shoring up the old shelter: pulling up palmetto plants from the hummocks and dragging logs across the clearing, fixing the largest of the abandoned cabins into a place that was livable, for all of them.

He liked the way they began to look at him, on about the tenth day of their being there, and he did not feel seventy-seven. He slid down out of the tree, walked across the clearing toward the largest woman, the one he had had his eye on, and took her hand, hugged her, felt her broad fat back, the backs of her legs, which were sweaty, and then her behind, while she giggled.

All that week, as the weather changed, they came drifting in, women from town, sometimes carrying lawn chairs, always wild-eyed and tentative when they saw the alligators and catfish, the others moving around naked in camp, brown as the earth itself—but then they would recognize someone, and would move out into the clearing with wonder, and a disbelief at having escaped. A breeze might be stirring, and dry colored hardwood leaves, ash and hickory, and oak and beech, orange and gold, would tumble down into the clearing, spill around their ankles, and the leaves made empty scraping sounds when the women walked through them, shuffling, looking up at the spinning fish.

At night they would sit around the fire and eat the dripping juiciness of the alligators, roasted: fat, from the tails, sweet, glistening on their hands, their faces; running down to their elbows. They smeared it on their backs, their breasts, to keep the mosquitoes away. Nights smelled of wood smoke. They could see the stars above their trees, above the shadows of their catches.

The women had all screamed and run into the woods, in different directions, the first time Buzbee leaped into the water after an alligator; but now they all gathered close and applauded and chanted an alligator-catching song they had made up that had few vowels, whenever he wrestled them. But that first time they thought he had lost his mind: he had rolled around and around in the thick gray-white slick mud, down by the bank, jabbing the young alligator with his pocketknife again and again, perforating it and muttering savage dog noises, until they could no longer tell which was which, except for the jets of blood that spurted out of the alligator's fat belly—but after he had killed the reptile, and rinsed off in the shallows, and come back across the oxbow, wading in knee-deep water, carrying it in his arms, a four-footer, his largest ever, he was smiling, gap-toothed, having lost two in the fight, but he was also erect, proud, and ready for love. It was the first time they had seen that.

The one he had hugged went into the hut after him.

The other women walked around the alligator carefully, and poked sticks at it, but also glanced toward the hut and listened, for the brief and final end of the small thrashings, the little pleasure, that was going on inside, the confirmation, and presently it came: Buzbee's goatish bleats, and the girl's too, which made them look at one another with surprise, wonder, interest, and speculation.

"It's those berries he's eatin," said one, whose name was Onessimius. Oney.

"They tastes bad," said Tasha.

"They makes your pee turn black," said Oney.

They looked at her with caution.

*J*esse didn't have the money for a car, or even for an old tractor.

He bought a used lawn-mower engine instead, for fifteen dollars; he found some old plywood in a dry abandoned barn. He scrounged some wheels, and stole a fan belt from a car rotting in a field, with bright wildflowers growing out from under the hood and mice in the back seat. He made a go-cart, and put a long plastic antenna with an orange flag, a banner, on the back of it that reached high into the sky, so that any motorists coming would see it.

But there was never any traffic. He sputtered and coughed up the hills, going one, two miles an hour: then coasting down, a slight breeze in his face. He didn't wear his biking helmet, and the breeze felt good.

It took him an hour to get to Hollingsworth's sometimes; he carried a sack lunch with him, apples and potato chips, and ate, happily, as he drove.

He started out going over to Hollingsworth's in the mid-morning, and always tried to come back in the early afternoon, so that the bikers would not see him; but it got more and more to where he didn't care, and finally, he just came and went as he pleased, waving happily when he saw them. But they never waved back. Sometimes the one who had replaced him, the trailing one, would spit water from his thermos bottle onto the top of Jesse's head as he rushed past; but they were gone quickly, almost as fast as they had appeared, and soon he was no longer thinking about them. They were gone.

Cottonwoods. Rabbits. Fields. It was still summer, it seemed it would always be summer; the smell of hay was good, and dry. All summer, they cut hay in the fields around him.

The go-cart rumbled along, carrying him; threatening to stop on the hill, but struggling on. He was a slow movement of color going up the hills, with everything else in his world motionless; down in the fields, black Angus grazed, and cattle egrets stood behind them and on their backs. Crows sat in the dead limbs of trees, back in the woods, watching him, watching the cows, waiting for fall.

He would reach Hollingsworth's, and the old man would be waiting, like a child: wanting his father back. It was a ritual. Hollingsworth would wave, tiredly: hiding in his heart the delight at seeing another person.

Jesse would wave back as he drove up into the gravel drive. He would grunt and pull himself up out of the little go-cart, and go over to the Coke machine.

The long slide of the bottle down the chute; the rattle, and *clunk*.

They'd sit on the porch, and Hollingsworth would begin to talk.

"I saw one of those explode in a man's hand," he said, pointing to the bottle Jesse was drinking. "Shot a sliver of glass as long as a knife up into his forearm, all the way. He didn't feel a thing: he just looked at it, and then walked around, pointing to it, showing everybody . . ."

Hollingsworth remembered everything that had ever happened to him. He told Jesse everything.

Jesse would stir after the second or third story. He couldn't figure it out; he couldn't stand to be too close to Hollingsworth, to listen to him for more than twenty or thirty minutes—he hated it after that point—but always, he went back; every day.

It was as if he got full, almost to the point of vomiting; but then he got hungry again.

He sat on the porch and drank Cokes, and ate cans and cans of whatever Hollingsworth had on the shelf: yams, mushrooms, pickles, deviled ham—and he knew, as if it were an equation on a blackboard, that his life had gone to hell—he could see it in the size of his belly resting between his soft legs—but he didn't know what to do.

There was a thing that was not in him anymore, and he did not know where to go to find it.

Oney was twenty-two and had had a bad husband. She still had the stiches in her forehead: he had thrown a chair at her, because she had called him a lard-ass, which he was. The stitches in the center of her head looked like a third eyebrow, with the eye missing. She hadn't heard about the old days of yellow fever and what it could do to one person, or everyone.

One night, even though she slept in Buzbee's arms, and even though the night was still and warm, she began to shiver wildly. And then two days later, again, she shivered and shook all night, and then two days later, a third time: it was coming every forty-eight hours, which was how it had been when Buzbee and Hollingsworth had had it.

Oney had been pale to begin with, and was turning, as if with the leaves, yellow, right in front of them: a little brighter yellow each day. All of the women began to eat the berries, slowly at first, and then wolfishly, watching Oney as they ate them.

They had built a little palmetto coop for their remaining chickens, which were laying regularly, and they turned them out, three small white magicians moving through the woods in search of bugs, seeds, and berries, and the chickens split up and wandered in different directions, and Buzbee and all the women split up, too, and followed them single file, at a distance, waiting for the chickens to find more berries, but somehow two of the chickens got away from them, escaped, and when they came back to camp, with the one remaining white chicken, a large corn snake was in the rooster's cage and was swallowing him, with only his thrashing feet showing: the snake's mouth hideous and wide, eyes wide and unblinking, mouth stretched into a laugh, as if he was enjoying the meal. Buzbee killed the snake, but the rooster died shortly after being pulled back out.

Oney screamed and cried, and shook until she was spitting up more black blood, when they told her they were going to take her back into town, and she took Buzbee's pocketknife and pointed it between her breasts and swore she would kill herself if they tried to make her go back to Luscious. And so they let her stay, and fed her their dwindling berry supply, and watched the stars, the sunset, and hoped for a hard and cold winter and an early freeze, but the days stayed warm, though the leaves were changing on schedule, and always, they looked for berries, and began experimenting, too, with the things Buzbee and Hollingsworth had tried so many years ago: cedar berries, mushrooms, hickory nuts, acorns. They smeared grease from the fish and alligators over every inch of their bodies, and kept a fire going again, at all times.

None of the women would go back to town. And none of them other than Oney had started spitting up blood or shivering yet. Ozzie, Buzbee's first woman, had missed her time.

And Buzbee sat up in the trees and looked down on them often, and stopped eating his berries, unbeknownst to them, so that there would be more for them. The alligators hung from the trees like dead insurgents, traitors to a way of life. They weren't seeing any more in the bayou, and he wasn't catching nearly as many fish. The fall was coming, and winter beyond that. The animals knew it first. Nothing could prevent its coming, or even slow its approach: nothing they could do would matter. Buzbee felt fairly certain that he had caught enough alligators.

*H*ollingsworth and Jesse made another approach a week later. Hollingsworth had the lariat and was wearing cowboy boots and a hat. Jesse was licking a Fudgicle.

Buzbee, in his tree, spotted them and jumped down.

"Shit," said Hollingsworth when they got to the camp. "He saw us coming again."

"He runs away," said Jesse, nodding. They could see the muddy slide marks where Buzbee and the women had scrambled out on the other side. The dark wall of trees, a wall.

"I've got an idea," said Hollingsworth.

They knew where Buzbee and the women were getting their firewood from: a tremendous logjam, with driftwood stacked all along the banks, not far from the camp.

Hollingsworth and Jesse went and got shovels, and some old mattresses from the dump, and came back and dug pits: huge, deep holes, big enough to bury cars, big enough to hold a school bus.

"I saw it on a Tarzan show," said Hollingsworth. His heart was burning; both of the men were dripping with sweat. It was the softest, richest dirt in the world, good and loose and black and easy to move, but they were out of shape and it took them all day. They sang as they dug, to keep Buzbee and the women at bay, hemmed in, back in the trees.

Buzbee and the women sat up on their branches, swatting at mosquitoes, and listened, and wondered what was going on.

"Row, row, row your boat!" Jesse shouted as he dug, his big belly wet, like a melon. Mopping his brow; his face streaked, with dirt and mud. He remembered the story about the pioneers who went crazy alone and dug their own graves: standing at the edge, then, and doing it.

"Oh, say—can—you—see," Hollingsworth brayed, "by the dawn's earl—lee—light?"

Back in the trees, the women looked at Buzbee for an explanation. They knew it was his son.

"He was born too early," he said weakly. "He has never been right."

"He misses you," said Oney. "That boy wants you to come home."

Buzbee scowled and looked down at his toes, hunkered on the branch, and held on fiercely, as if the tree had started to sway.

"That boy don't know *what* he wants," he said.

When Hollingsworth and Jesse had finished the pits, they spread long branches over them, then scattered leaves and twigs over the branches.

"We'll catch the whole tribe of them," Hollingsworth cackled.

Jesse nodded. He was faint, and didn't know if he could make it all the way back out or not. He wondered vaguely what Buzbee and the women would be having for supper.

The mosquitoes were vicious; the sun was going down. Owls were beginning to call.

"Come on," said Hollingsworth. "We've got to get out of here."

Jesse wanted to stay. But he felt Hollingsworth pull on his arm; he let himself be led away.

Back in the woods, up in the tree, Oney began to shiver, and closed her eyes, lost consciousness, and fell. Buzbee leaped down and gathered her up, held her tightly, and tried to warm her with his body.

"They gone," said a woman named Vesuvius. The singing had gone away when it got dark, as had the ominous sound of digging.

There was no moon, and it was hard, even though they were familiar with it, to find their way back to camp.

They built fires around Oney, and two days later she was better. But they knew it would come again.

"Look at what that fool boy of yours has done," Tasha said the next day. A deer had fallen into one of the pits and was leaping about, uninjured, trying to get free.

Buzbee said his favorite curse word, a new one that Oney had told him, "Fuckarama," and they tried to rope the deer, but it was too wild: it would not let them get near.

"We could stone it," Tasha said, but not with much certainty; and they all knew they could not harm the deer, trapped as it was, so helpless.

Then at dusk they saw Oney's husband moving through the woods, perilously close to their camp, moving through the gray trees, stalking their woods with a shotgun.

They hid in their huts and watched, hoping he would not look down the hill and see their camp, not see the alligators hanging.

Oney was whimpering. Her husband's dark, slow shape moved cautiously about, but the light was going fast: that darkness of purple, all light being drawn away. He faded; he disappeared; it was dark. Then, in the night, they heard a yell and a blast, and then the quietest silence they had ever known.

It was a simple matter burying him in the morning. They hadn't thought of letting the deer out that way. They had not thought of filling in the pit partially, so that the deer could walk out.

"You will get better," they told Oney. She believed them. On the days in which she did not have the fever, she believed them. There was still, though, the memory of it.

It was escapable. Some people lived through it and survived. It didn't get everyone. They didn't all just lie down and die, those who got it.

She loved old Buzbee, on her good days. She laughed, and slept with him, rolled with him, and put into the back of her mind what had happened before, and what would be happening again.

Her teeth, when she was laughing, pressing against him, clutching him, shutting her eyes. She would fight to keep it in the back of her mind, and to keep it behind her.

*J*esse rode out to Hollingsworth's in the go-cart. He took a back road, a different route. The air was cooler, it seemed that summer could be ending, after all, and he felt like just getting out and seeing the country again. It was a road he had always liked to ride on, with or without the pack, back when he had been racing, and he had forgotten how fresh it had been, how it had tasted, just to look at it. He drove through a tunnel of trees; a pasture, on the other side of the trees, a stretch of pastel green, a smear of green, with charcoal cattle standing in it, and white egrets at their sides, pressed an image into the sides of his slow-moving vision. It was almost cold down in the creek bottom, going through the shade, so slowly.

He smiled and gave a small whoop, and waved a fist in the air. The light on the other side of the trees, coming down onto the field, was the color of gold smoke.

He had a sack of groceries with him, behind the engine, and he reached back and got a sandwich and a canned drink.

*T*hey went to check the traps, the pits, flushing Buzbee's troops back into the swamp, as ever.

"I'd hoped we could have caught them all," said Hollingsworth. His eyes were pale, mad, and he wanted to dig more holes.

"Look," he said. "They buried my mattress." He bent down on the fresh mound and began digging at it with his hands; but he gave up shortly, and looked around blankly, as if forgetting why he had been digging in the first place.

Buzbee and the women were getting angry at being chased so often, so regularly. They sat in the trees and waited. Some of the women said nothing, but hoped, to themselves, that Hollingsworth and Jesse would forget where some of the pits lay, and would stumble in.

*J*esse and Hollingsworth sat on Hollingsworth's porch.

"You don't talk much," Hollingsworth said, as if noticing for the first time.

Jesse said nothing. It was getting near the twenty-minute mark. He had had two Cokes and a package of Twinkies. He was thinking about how it had been, when he had been in shape, and riding with the others, the pack: how his old iron bike had been a traitor some days, and his legs had laid down and died, and he had run out of wind—but how he had kept going, anyway, and how eventually—though only for a little while—it had gotten better.

The bikers rode past. They were moving so fast. Hills were nothing to them. They had light bikes, expensive ones, and the climbs were only excuses to use the great strength of their legs. The wind in their faces, and pressing back against their chests, was but a reason and a direction, for a feeling: it was something to rail against, and defeat, or be defeated by—but it was tangible. Compared to some things, the wind was actually tangible.

They shouted encouragement to one another as they jockeyed back and forth, sharing turns, breaking the wind for each other.

"*I*'m ready," Hollingsworth told Jesse on his next visit, a few days later.

He was jumping up and down like a child.

"I'm ready, I'm ready," Hollingsworth sang. "Ready for anything."

He had a new plan. All he had been doing was thinking: trying to figure out a way to get something back.

So Jesse rode his bike to town to get the supplies they would need: an extra lariat and rope for trussing him up with; they figured he would be senile and wild. Muzzles for the dogs. Jesse rode hard, for a fat man.

The wind was coming up. It was the first week in September. The hay was baled, stood in tall rolls, and the fields looked tame, civilized, smoothed: flattened.

They muzzled the dogs and put heavy leashes on their collars, and started out across the field with a kerosene lantern and some food and water.

When they had crossed the field—half running, half being dragged by the big dogs' eagerness—and came to the edge of the woods, they were halted by the mosquitoes, which rose up in a noisy dark cloud and fell upon them like soft fingers. The dogs turned back, whining in their muzzles, yelping, instinct warning them of the danger of these particular mosquitoes, and they kept backing away, back into the field, and would not go down into the swamp.

So Hollingsworth and Jesse camped back in the wind of the pasture, in the cool grass, and waited for daylight. They could smell the smoke from Buzbee's camp, but could see nothing, the woods were so dark. There was a quarter-moon, and it came up so close to them, over the trees, that they could see the craters.

Hollingsworth talked. He talked about the space program. He asked Jesse if this wasn't better than riding his old bike. They shared a can of Vienna sausage. Hollingsworth talked all night. Chuck-will's-widows called, and bullbats thumped around in the grass, not far from their small fire: flinging themselves into the grass and flopping around as if mourning; rising again, flying past, and then twisting and slamming hard, without a cry, as if pulled down by a sudden force. As if their time was up. All around them, the bullbats flew like this, twisting and then diving into the ground, until it seemed to Jesse that they were trying to send a message: Go back, go back.

And he imagined, as he tried not to listen to Hollingsworth, that the bikers he had ridden with, the Frenchmen, were asleep, or making love to soft women, or eating ice-cream cones.

A light drizzle woke Hollingsworth and Jesse and the dogs in the morning, and they stood up and stretched, and then moved on the camp. Crickets were chirping quietly in the soft rain, and the field was steaming. There wasn't any more smoke from the fire. The dogs had been smelling Buzbee and his camp all night, and were nearly crazed: their chests swelled and strained like barrels of apples, like hearts of anger, and they jumped and twisted and tugged against their leashes, pulling Hollingsworth and Jesse behind them in a stumbling run through the wet grasses.

Froth came from their muzzles, their rubbery lips. Their eyes were wild. They were too hard to hold. They pulled free of their leashes, and raced, silently, like the fastest thing in the world, accelerating across the field and into the woods, straight for the camp, the straightest thing that ever was.

*J*esse bought a bike with the reward money: a French bicycle, a racer, with tires that were thinner than a person's finger held sideways. It could fly. It was light blue, like an old man's eyes.

Hollingsworth had chained Buzbee to the porch: had padlocked the clasp around his ankle with thirty feet of chain. It disgusted Jesse, but he was even more disgusted by his own part in the capture, and by the size of his stomach, his loss of muscle.

He began to ride again: not with the pack, but by himself.

He got fast again, as he had thought he could. He got faster than he had been before, faster than he had ever imagined, and bought a stopwatch and raced against himself, timing himself, riding up and down the same roads over and over again.

Sometimes, riding, he would look up and see Buzbee out on the porch, standing, with Hollingsworth sitting behind him, talking. Hollingsworth would wave wildly.

One night, when Jesse got in from his ride, the wind had shifted out of the warm west and was from the north, and it felt serious, and in it, after Jesse had bathed and gotten in bed, was the thing, not for the first time, but the most insistent that year, that made Jesse get back out of bed, where he was reading, and go outside and sit on the steps beneath his porch light. He tried to read.

Moths fell down off the porch light's bulb, brushed his shoulders, landed on the pages of his book, spun, and flew off, leaving traces of magic. And the wind began to stir harder. Stars were all above him, and they glittered and flashed in the wind. They seemed to be challenging him, daring him to see what was true.

Two miles away, up on the hill, back in the trees, the A.M.E. congregation was singing. He couldn't see the church lights, but for the first time that year he could hear the people singing, the way he could in the winter, when there were no leaves on the trees and when the air was colder, more brittle, and sounds carried. He could never hear the words, just the sad moaning that sometimes, finally, fell away into pleasure.

He stood up on the porch and walked out into the yard, the cool grass, and tried some sit-ups. When he was through, he lay back, sweating slightly, breathing harder, and he watched the stars, but they weren't as bright, it seemed, and he felt as if he had somehow failed them, had not done the thing expected or, rather, the thing demanded.

When he woke up in the morning, turned on his side in the yard, lying out in the grass like an animal, the breeze was still blowing and the light of the day was gold, coming out of the pines on the east edge of his field.

He sat up, stiffly, and for a moment forgot who he was, what he did, where he was—it was the breeze moving across him, so much cooler suddenly—and then he remembered, it was so simple, that he was supposed to ride.

*I*t was early November. It was impossible to look at the sky, at the trees, at the cattle in the fields even, and not know that it was November. The clasp around Buzbee's ankle was cold; his legs were getting stronger from pulling the chain around with him. He stood out on the porch, and the air, when he breathed deeply, went all the way down into his chest: he felt good. He felt like wrestling an alligator.

He had knocked Hollingsworth to the ground, tried to get him to tell him where the key was. But Hollingsworth, giggling, with his arm twisted behind his back—the older man riding him, breathing hard but steadily, pushing his son's face into the floor—had told Buzbee that he had thrown the key away. And Buzbee, knowing his son, his poisoned loneliness, knew that it was so.

The chain was too big to break or smash.

*S*ometimes Buzbee cried, looking at it. He felt as if he could not breathe; it was as if he were being smothered. It was like a thing was about to come to a stop.

*H*e watched the field all the time. Jesse raced by, out on the road, checking his watch, looking at it, holding it in one hand, pedaling hard: flying, it seemed.

Buzbee heard Hollingsworth moving behind him, coming out to gab. It was like being in a cell.

Buzbee could see the trees, the watery blur of them, on the other side of the field.

"Pop," said Hollingsworth, ready with a story.

Pop, my ass, thought Buzbee bitterly. He wanted to strangle his own son.

He had so wanted to make a getaway—to have an escape, clean and free.

He looked out at the field, remembering what it had been like with the women, and the alligators, and he thought how he would be breaking free again, shortly, for good.

This time, he knew, he would get completely away.

The blue line of trees, where he had been with the women, wavered and flowed, in watercolor blotches, and there was a dizziness high in his forehead. He closed his eyes and listened to his mad son babble, and he prepared, and made his plans.

When he opened his eyes, the road was empty in front of him. Jesse was gone: a streak, a flash: already gone.

It was as if he had never been there.

Buzbee narrowed his eyes and gripped the porch railing, squinted at the trees, scowled, and tried to figure another way out.

.

CATS AND STUDENTS,
BUBBLES AND ABYSSES

I got a roommate, he's tall and skinny, when we get in arguments he says "I went to Millsaps," uses the word like what he thinks a battering ram sounds like. He's a real jerk, I could break both his arms just like that! if I wanted to, I've got a degree in English Literature from Jackson State, I was the only white on campus, I can't use "I went to Jackson State" like a battering ram, but I can break both his arms. I got a doctorate, it took me three more years. I teach out at the junior-college— Freshman Comp, Heroes and Heroines of Southern Literature, Contemporary Southern Lit, Contemporary Northern Lit, that sort of crap. Piss-Ant studied geology, "pre-oil" he calls it facetiously, makes quite a ton of money, I swear I could tear an arm off his thin frail body and beat him over the head with it, I'm 5'6" tall, eighteen inches shorter than he but I'm thirty pounds heavier, an even 195, I played for the Tiges three years and can dead lift 700 pounds and run a marathon in under three hours six minutes.

I swear one of these days I'm gonna kill him, he may have gone to Millsaps (" 'Saps," he calls it, there, you hate him too) but he doesn't know how to use a Kleenex. Instead he just goes around making these enormously tall wet sniffles, if you could hear just one of them you would first shiver and then you too would want to kill him. If they catch me and bring me to court I suppose I can always bring that up in the trial, I must go out and buy a tape recorder first thing tomorrow but first the cat needs feeding, he's a violent little sunuvabitch.

I will tell you about the cat after I tell you what I did in Arkansas.

Back when I was a hot-shot cruising timber for Weyerhaeuser I had seven hillbillies and a nigger working under me, I told them where to cut the big trees, diameter breast height and all that mess; I had lots of money then but I quit that job. I got tired of seeing all those trees falling. I'm poor now but at least I got the hell out of the tree-killing business. Perhaps I could do him in in his bed, while he slept. I could cut his throat with a razor, make it look like he had an accident shaving.

His name is W.C. He's the only thing I like about Jackson, Mississippi. He's a bad-ass: he only eats live pigeons. You know how cats can be finicky. I have to trap them for him under the interstate, off Fortification. The first time I was driving through Jackson I saw that street sign and about fell out of the car, I thought they had a street called Fornification. Everything has been sort of downhill since.

Nights, when I'm not lifting, I'm working on a fourth degree, in Computer Science, out at the junior college, all my colleagues know this and think I'm thinking about leaving for a better-paying job in a state not southern in nationality. This worries them, I can tell, especially Slater. They don't want me to leave, we generally have a pretty well-knit little group of us that drinks and parties and carries on and bad-mouths the students together, none of the rest of the faculty lifts but despite this I am still a pretty well-liked guy, they think just because I keep a road map of Montana rolled up in my bottom desk drawer that that is where I want to go next.

Used to be people would only invite me over to their house when they were moving, to help them lift the refrigerator and the piano, you know, but would forget when it was time for the delicate stuff like waxing the cabinets or something, they'd invite damn near everybody except me. A person less sensitive than I might have been insulted, and left, moved away from the south. Not I. They just needed telling. In the noble West, where I used to live before I reached puberty, it was manly and virtuous not to tell people about yourself, but to let them find out. It made it better that way. But not in Mississippi. In the south, you were supposed to tell them. They held it against you if you didn't, because it meant you were trying to hide something from them, trying to deprive them of something more precious to them than food (which is plenty precious enough, the south has lots of pretty girls yes but there's a lot of awful fat ones too, oh well). I found out it was a mistake to deprive them of anything they could gossip about. Which is what you were doing if you didn't tell them about yourself. I mean everything: good, bad or indifferent. Tell all, do, do.

So.

Look here, I said when I had this figured out, figured out why they weren't inviting me to wax but instead only to move furniture. I am college educated. I have a degree from Jackson State. (I tried to say this like a battering ram.) Look here, I told them, I am a writer, almost.

They liked that. They started inviting me to wax cabinets, and other smart things. I was pleased. I had friends. I did not leave the south as others might have.

I did not tell you about that writing thing.

W.C. wouldn't like Montana. He'd freeze his ass off. But I don't tell them that: it is fun to think they think I'm thinking about leaving, and to tell me with knowing, understanding looks, to "hang in there" whenever we part company. They all think they know what I am going through, they think I hate the south like they do. It's not much but then not many places are. I know lots of people who have gotten brave and left, gone to Texas, California, South Dakota, and places like that. Many people are leaving the south.

The reason I room with a Piss-Ant is because he helps me pay for the rent. The reason I don't room with Slater is because he yells in his sleep—lashes out at the world, very loudly, curses and even wakes the neighbors sometimes. Shit! Shit! Damn! That kind of thing.

If you were wondering but were too shy to ask, then no, I've not had W.C. castrated, he's mean enough as it is, besides, I want to make sure there's as many of him around as possible. If all cats were like W.C. they wouldn't have a bad name, not at all. I keep a set of barbells up at my desk, and when students are reading or taking a test I sometimes do light pumping sets of Scott curls over the podium to keep my arms flushed. The wood creaks as I do this, a few of them look up occasionally and with interest but not many, they're mostly candy-asses and pansies, and are waiting for the scholarships to come through so they can go to Millsaps. W.C. would not like most of them.

Except for Robby. Robby is sort of my protégé. Even though I haven't ever done anything, he calls me his mentor. That's his only flaw, his only weakness: calling an unpublished writer his mentor, when any professor in the whole frotting world would have him on, but that's the kind of writer he is, or will be. He knows what he likes, and doesn't give a rat's ass about what anybody else thinks, he's a winner in every way but that one.

Robby is not waiting for a scholarship to come through so he can go to Millsaps.

He sometimes comes over on weekends, drinks beer with me and Slater, we talk about girls, watch TV, cook a lot, we eat quite well. Slater used to be a poet, he's nothing now, and he sort of looks on Robby and me with awe because we aren't nothing yet, we haven't given up yet, awed at me because I'm thirty-one and haven't given up yet, and at Robby because he's young and has potential.

Most people stop wanting to be a writer around the age of sixteen.

We expect Robby is stuck with the curse for life.

He, Robby, hasn't really written anything yet, not any stories or anything like that, but he can write the hell out of a sentence. He writes some of the best I've ever read, it's just that they aren't ever about anything. It's like he gets tired easily. Sometimes it makes Slater's and my stomachs hurt, we want so badly for him to write a whole story.

If he ever gets untracked and is able to write a whole story or a book even, say six or seven *thousand* sentences about the same thing, then the big boys up in New York are going to go nuts about him. Where did this gem come from? they will ask.

Jackson, Mississippi, Slater and I will tell them. We taught him. Would you like any more just like him? we will ask, kind of snottily, as if they grow on trees down here.

Slater teaches poetry, jazz appreciation, and an occasional

humanities workshop. He smokes marijuana, even in the daytime, and has a beard.

Slater, too, hates Millsaps.

*T*his is how we discovered Robby: we saw him walking down the hall one day with a copy of Henry James under his arm.

No one under thirty reads Henry James for no-good reason. Not unless they are interested in being a writer. Slater and I tailed him at a distance out to the parking lot, took down his license plate, and went back to the registrar's office with it. Found out where he lived, and went to visit him that night. Wore sports coats and tennis shoes, and took a six-pack of beer and W.C.

On his dresser, in his bedroom, Piss-Ant has this picture taken of him when he was a freshman in college, maybe the best he's ever looked. He's at some tight-ass social function, there are tablecloths on the tables and lots of people and the wineglasses are still empty and turned upside down on the tables, and Piss-Ant is sitting down in this picture, wearing an ascot and a shit-faced grin, looking somehow and for once very good in this picture, sitting down so no one can tell what a freak he is, and next to him is this absolutely dynamite woman, a real woman and not a girl. She's maybe twenty-five or twenty-seven to his nineteen, and she's wearing a sequiny dress with breasts spilling out all over the place, and her hair is sand-blonde, white almost, and there's lots of it; her hoop earrings are silver and glittering, Piss-Ant is grinning, he's so drunk his eyes are crossed, and he's got his arm around this piece of heaven, she's grinning too, laughing even, you can see her teeth even, she's laughing so much. . . .

She's got to be his mother, his sister, a cousin, a whore, something. . . . She can't just be his date for that night. He's too much of a Piss-Ant.

I didn't tell you this but when he talks he sounds like the recording of a deep-voiced Iranian talking through a long hollow cardboard tube played at 17 rpm instead of 33. Like he's about to run out of batteries at any time. Like what everything he has to say is just between you and him, something he's found out through his own incredible knowledge but is going to let you in on it too. He can say "I'm going to go to the bathroom" and make it sound like he expects everyone to stop what they are doing and record the event in some sort of black notebook or diary. Slater and I sure do hate that picture.

I guess the most weight I've ever lifted is the back end of Slater's car. Robby and Slater and I took it up to Oxford to look at Faulkner's old house out in the country one Sunday. We got sort of lost and got sort of stuck in the mud. We had a couple dozen watermelons and a keg of beer in the back, it was a hot Mississippi summer, we were going to have a picnic, and the jack sank down in the mud and got lost, but I lifted the back end up anyway, as if all that beer and watermelon weren't in the back seat at all, and Slater and Robby tossed sticks and rocks under the tires and then I let it back down and we got inside, muddy as hell, and drove out of it, went on our way, off to picnic.

We'd bought the watermelons six-for-a-dollar in Neshoba County. We love a good deal. We got drunk and never did find Faulkner's old house, but it didn't matter. We had a great time and drove back down the Natchez Trace going about 20 mph and came creeping in around dawn and I came in still drunk and pissed in the cup Piss-Ant keeps by the side of his bed to keep his false teeth in, and then pretended to try to flush them by turning the lamp on and off, like I thought it was the toilet. "Ohrrorh," Piss-Ant said in the hollow Yankee toilet-tube voice, which is how he says "oh, no," when he found out. Slater and Robby and I laughed hard and long about it till we were in cramps, at lunch the next day.

I don't know if I told you this or not, Piss-Ant wears false teeth, he's twenty-seven but he's been wearing them ever since he was twenty-four, which is how old he was when I knocked them all out.

*A*nother time we tried to get Robby a girlfriend. Slater's divorced twice, with three kids and alimony payments, can't afford women anymore, and I scare them, this is fine with me, piss on them anyway if they don't like the way I shout and yell and rage and roar when I lift weights, what do I care if they don't like this, who needs them anyway? I'm not going to give up my lifting for anyone, besides my back is as hairy as an animal's, like a pelt, they don't like that either, but so what, I piss on them all from a considerable height, but Robby, he is different, he is young, he's good-looking too, he needs one, only he thinks they'd take up all his time, time he needs to be spending writing, you can see this great gulp slide up in his throat when he sees one is getting serious about him, you can see his eyes widen. He is forever getting up and leaving the room early at parties, and afterwards all the single girls ask about him, and Slater and I will go drive by his apartment after the party, drive by slowly, and almost no matter what time it is, we will see his second-story light on, and know he is in there at his desk writing some more of those damn fine sentences, with maybe a half-empty bottle of wine on his desk, that's all he drinks, white wine, at age twenty he's already become something of an alcoholic, that's why we were trying to find him a girlfriend, same thing only not as rough on the body, but we weren't having a lot of luck.

So we went home and fed W.C. a pigeon and got a six-pack

out of the refrigerator and then after we had cleaned the feathers up we sat down in the den and thought about it. Piss-Ant was not in; he'd gone home to Gulfport for the weekend, and was visiting his mother or some damn thing. It was after midnight. Slater is dangerous after midnight.

We thought and drank beer for about an hour. I had to get another six-pack out. It was like a genius was in my living room when Slater mentioned Maribeth Hutchings.

Maribeth Hutchings had been in one of my contemporary lit classes about five years ago. She was a little older than Robby, but that wasn't important. What was important was this: Maribeth had an uncle who was a writer. A real writer. He'd written three books, one of them had won an award even, and then he'd moved to Montana to write.

Another desperate Southerner, done escaped at his first chance.

Maribeth didn't write, but no matter: we could tell Robby she did. We'd never talked about it but we knew Robby well enough to know this: that if he did by some slip of self-discipline allow himself to become interested in a girl, she would have to be a writer herself, or at least be related to one.

It took us about three days to track this writer's niece down; when we found her, she was an accountant for an oil company.

She still entertained no thoughts of writing. She liked numbers. She was pleased by money, and the camaraderie of office life. We saw the diploma in her office. Noticed, regrettably, that she had finally ended up going to Millsaps. But Slater and I looked at each other. These things can be overcome, Slater's eyes said. I nodded. She was about twenty-six years old. She was beautiful. She was making about $70,000 a year. We sat down and told her our plan. We had even brought a picture of Robby, and a Big Chief tablet with some of his better sentences typed out on it, numbered one through ten, like commandments.

She glanced impatiently at the list, then asked us to leave.

I do not think she liked number six, the one about the dry leaf that blows hollow and forlorn down the empty canyon. We left.

So Robby remained hornate. No nooky for him, not till he becomes an accomplished writer: that's his unspoken vow, we can tell. He's friendly enough around us, he snatches up our b.s. about writers and writing like a man starved for the Secret, and he is all nose-to-the-grindstone and give-'em-hell damn-the-torpedoes when he sets about trying to write some more of his good sentences, but sometimes Slater and I have seen him alone on campus, walking, carrying his writing notebook in his arms, looking down at his feet as he walks, and he'll not know we're watching him, won't be aware anyone is watching him. He'll have this unGodly fierce scowl on his face—we're sure he doesn't realize it, he's not a mean student—and we'll know what he's thinking about, and we'll know how his stomach is turning around inside and how he just wants to slam his books down on the sidewalk and thrust his arms up in the air and roar at the heavens till the clouds shatter and fall submissively in broken tinkling jigsaw pieces to the ground.

Like I said, Slater does it every night, in his sleep.

It's like there's this shell over Robby, this confining, restricting, elastic-like bubble; it's like he's got to write his way out of it.

Robby backs up, writes a sentence, writes two good sentences, hurls himself at the bubble, but the sentences aren't good enough, he bounces back, maybe lands on his butt. He gets up, dusts himself off, picks up his books, writes another sentence, hurls himself, bounces back, falls again. . . .

It's frustrating as hell, I'll tell you; at Robby's age, and with his talent and potential, it's pure hell.

Most of us get used to the bubble finally, just ignore it, and quit bouncing against it, cease to hurl ourselves recklessly against the thing, and settle for moving around cautiously within its limits as best we can.

Only at night, asleep, or sometimes when we have been drinking too much, do we ever dream about how clean and crisp the air tastes on the outside of that bubble, and how for many years we labored to taste that air; only in our dreams do we ever reach for it now: asleep, or drunk.

But Robby's still young: he's imagining that he's suffocating. He thinks he's got to get into that air outside the bubble or die. He thinks it's like a curse.

He's right, in a way, but the curse of it is this: it's not death that will come if he is unable to break out of the bubble, but something worse. He will continue to live.

*U*sually I get pretty sick of grading papers in my Freshman Comp class. I usually don't even do it; I just throw them away, and tell the students I'm still looking at them, really pondering over them and will probably have to return them in the mail next semester or something. I've got about a dozen bushels of them wadded up in the attic, I bring them down and use them to start the fires in the fireplace with each winter, good God they are awful, I sometimes read a page or two as I unrumple them and feed them to the fire; they make my stomach cramp and my breath come fast and shallow. Piss-Ant says I am irresponsible and maybe I am, but let me tell you these papers are awful. Having Robby write here amongst the students at the j.c. is like turning a cave man loose in the Stone Age with a real steel sword, can you imagine the luxurious piggishness it would afford him, the only one in a world still made of stones? Robby is a steel sword among stones. Invincible.

To the extent that a sword will take you. The editors up north aren't yet impressed with Robby, and Slater and I can't really blame them, for it's stories people like to read, not just sentences, but one of these days he is coming out of that bubble, he will come slashing his way out of it like a claw-raking demon, like an axe-wielding barbarian, and then people will know about him and he will become one of Them. Robby Starkley, writer. Not author, but writer.

If he can hang tough, He's only twenty.

We try to steer him away from stories of Anne Tyler, who won the Anne Flexner Creative Writing Prize at Duke and graduated when she was nineteen, who had published two novels by the time she was twenty-four. Of John Irving, who spent three years polishing his first novel at the Writers' Workshop in Iowa before finally having it published at the advanced age of twenty-five.

John Gardner spent fifteen years flinging himself against the bubble before he got out. He's dead now, of course, died three Septembers ago, it killed him, getting out did, but at least he did get out.

But still, we wish he'd get a girlfriend, a really beautiful one, elegant even, something to buffer the sting a little in case he doesn't make it, or at least a pal to bum around with his own age, instead of running around with two old ex-writers all the time. It's like he's sacrificing the present: it's like he's gambling everything on the future, and if he misses, he'll suddenly look up and be thirty-five or forty and there won't be a thing behind him: nothing but an empty, gaping abyss. He'll fall back into it.

Bubbles, abysses . . . I think about these things a lot, worry about Robby a little every day. God how I want him to make it.

In the summers, Slater and W.C. and I often drive down to

the coast for a day, and lie out on towels on the beach in the sand under the sun smelling of coconut and wear sunglasses, and drink cold beer with sand grains stuck on the wetness of the cans and sit up sometimes with one elbow propped and watch the girls, and listen to the cries of seagulls and the sound of the waves and the big fancy radios and generally do nothing all day. W.C. chases hermit crabs, hides in the sea oats and watches people, and it's really all right.

*S*later lashes out at the world in his dreams, at night, and in the day, alone in an empty room with mirrors, I lift heavy weights again and again until my eyes swim in black pools of pain and gold flashes streak through my arms and shoulders.

And Robby writes.

In my own dreams at night, and rehearsing in front of the mirror, this is sometimes what I feel like telling Piss-Ant when I see him come driving up in the piss-ant little MG with the top down and a pretty girl in the seat. Do not think I could not have studied pre-oil myself, you little bastard, do not think either Slater or myself could not have studied it and gotten a job in it and done damn good, because we could have, you brown-nosing candy-assing death-loving piss-anting bubble-bound little coward.

We try to keep Robby away from Piss-Ant as much as possible.

JUGGERNAUT

When I was seventeen, Kirby and I had a teacher who was crazy. This happened in the last year before Houston got big and unlivable.

Big Ed, we called him: Eddie Odom. Mr. Odom. He taught geometry as an after-thought; his stories were what he got excited about. Class began at nine o'clock. By nine-twenty, he would be winded, tired of sines and cosines, and he would turn to the clock in a way that almost aroused sympathy—so tired!—and he would try to last his lecture out for another five or ten minutes, before going into his stories. The thrill that Kirby and I felt when he lurched into these stories following a half-hearted geometrical lecture—there would be no warning whatsoever, we would suddenly be listening to something as fantastically wild and free as geometry was boring, and we wouldn't have done anything to earn it, we'd find ourselves just pulled into it, in the middle of it, and enjoying.

He had lived in Walla Walla, Washington, for a while, he told us, the first day we were in his class, and while there he had had a pet lion, and had to move back to Houston after the lion stabbed a child in the chest with its tail.

Houston, he told us, was the only town in the country that was zoned and ordinanced properly, so that a man could do what he wanted, as he wanted. He paused for about five minutes after he said this, and looked at us, one by one, going down the rows in alphabetical order, to make sure we had understood him.

Simmons, Simonini; Kirby and I watched him sweep down the aisles, student by student. There was a tic in his eyebrow that flared alarmingly when he passed over Laura DeCastagnola, who was tiny, olive-skinned, exuberant and good-calved. Possibly he was trying to be a hero for her. All the rest of us were.

Big Ed was graying, in his late forties, possibly even fifty, slope-shouldered, of medium height—literally taller than half of us, and shorter than the rest—and he moved with an awkward power: as if perhaps once he had had this very great strength that had somehow been taken away: an injury inside, to some set of nerves, which still retained the strength, but did not allow him to use it. Like a loaded pistol, or a car parked on the hill without an emergency brake—that was the impression he gave Kirby and me.

The child in Washington had been a punk, he told us, ten years old, and foul-mouthed, but had lived anyway.

"All female lions have a claw hidden in their tail," said Big Ed—and then stopped and locked the whole class with a look as if the last thing he would ever have expected was snickers and laughs. "No, it's true."

Kirby and I listened raptly; it was only the rest of the class which was disgusted by his callousness. Kirby and I were willing to give him that doubt. It was then and is so today still our major fault. Nothing will get you into trouble so deep or as sad as faith.

While the rest of the class hesitated, froze, and drew back from Big Ed—not understanding, but reacting, an instinct they felt—Kirby and I ignored it, this avoidance instinct, shy of it, that growing-up spring, and plunged after, and into his stories. We didn't look left or right. No one could be that crazy. Besides, we were frightened of growing up.

The point of the story had to be that female lions had claws in their tails. The other was all a smokescreen. No one *truly* believed a ten-year old boy deserved to be stabbed by a lion.

He encouraged us to go down to the zoo and somehow manage to slip a hand in through the bars of the lion cage, behind them, and find out.

"It's hidden, deep under all that fringe. It's as sharp as a nail, and like a stinger, only curved: just another claw. My guess is it's left over, from a time we don't know about, when lions used to swing from the trees, like monkeys."

Feet would shift and books would be closed or moved around, when the talk edged towards the ludicrous, as it often did.

The more adult-bound of the class would even sigh, and look out the window—it was harsh spring, and green, the lawn mowers clugging thick and choking every few yards with rich wet dark grass, and its smell of fermentation—and we all had cars, that spring, as it was Houston, and Texas, and there weren't any of us who weren't handsome, or beautiful, or going places, or popular, or sure of it all. Except Kirby and me. And Big Ed would stop, slowly but also too, somehow, bolt-like—that nerve again, perhaps—his eyebrows were arched and furry, and went all the way across—and he would squint his eyes at Cam Janse, shock white bleach haired, and lanky, sun-glasses, or at Tucker White, whose lips were big and curved, like a girl's, and who *had* all the girls— who would be pretending with these adult sighs and glances out the window that they would both be glad when the discussion got back to the more interesting topic of geometry—and so then Big Ed would assign about two or three hundred problems, over things we'd not even learned yet.

When the bell would ring, the boys sitting behind and next to Laura DeCastagnola were slower getting out of their desks than the rest of the class, and they walked oddly, holding their books at a ridiculous angle, close in and below their waists, as if aching from an unseen cramp. She had a jawline that you wanted to trace with your fingers. There was never a flatter, smoother region of face than that below her intelligent cheekbones. She made A's, and she was nice, and quiet, but she laughed like a monkey.

She would explode with her laughs, giggling and choking on them. She wore her cheerleader's dress on Friday. The blouse white without sleeves, the skirt gold. There were white socks. She wasn't sweet on anybody. She was everybody's sister. When she went to the football games and cheered, she was unique, standing under that vamp of mercury haze gold twinkling light—a huge vacuum cleaner could have sucked it and all of its charged magic away, leaving us only under a night sky out in the Texas prairie—unique in that she was always conscious of the score, and cared that we won, more so than about the party afterwards.

"Go, KEN!" she would scream. Ken Sims, breaking free, getting to the sideline and racing down it in his gallop, running all wrong, feet getting tangled up, no forward body lean, a white farmboy from Arkansas, the leading scorer in the city that year. Calves like bird's legs. If Laura *had* had a boyfriend, it would have been Ken.

We'd see Big Ed, too, up in the stands, with his scarecrow wife, who looked to be ten or fifteen years older than he, and was seven feet tall, with one of those small bug-like dark rubies in the center of her forehead, though she was not Pakistani, but pale, looked as pale and American as Wichita, or Fort Dodge. Big Ed would be watching Laura as if no one else was down there, and while the rest of the stadium would be jumping up and down, moving, orchestrating to Laura's leaps—her back to us, when Ken was running—Big Ed would be standing there, as motionless as a totem.

I would nudge Kirby and point, secretly, up to Big Ed—his eyes would be riveted on her, his mouth slightly open, as if he was about to say something—and we would stop watching the game for a second, and be troubled by it. We didn't see how he could be thinking it: lusting after a student, and such a nice one.

And down on the field, Ken, or Mark, or Amos, would score. Our band would play that brassy little elephant song. And Laura would leap, and kick, and throw her arms up and out. We were on our way to an undefeated season, that senior year. Who would want to lose any games in their last year? So we didn't. And we thought we were ready for that step, going out into the real world, and beyond.

It was such a time of richness that there was more than one hockey team, even—the struggling Aeros weren't enough. They played in the Spectrum, and were nothing more than an oddity, like so much else in the town at that time, and destined for a short life. The only reason at all people went to see them was because Gordie Howe, the Canadian legend, was making a comeback at the age of 48, and was both playing for and managing the team, and his two sons were playing for the Aeros with him, and he was scoring goals, and winning games.

But the other team was one that no one knew about, a seedier, underground version of the Aeros, and they played far out on the west end of town, on the warped and ratty ice rink in Houston. It was out on the highway that led into the rice fields, and tickets to the game were only fifty cents. The name of the team was the Juggernauts, and they played anybody.

We were driving then, had been for a year. We were free. Kirby had a sandy blue Mercury, one of the Detroit old iron horses from the sixties that would throw you into its back seat if you accelerated hard, and we would, on Tuesdays and Thursdays, race out into the night, away from the city's suburban lights, and

we would pay with pennies, dimes and nickels—for Kirby and I
had vowed never to work—and we would grip our tickets and step
through the low doorway and go down the steps and into all the
light, to see the Juggernauts, on the arena that served as a children's skating rink in the day.

When we would get there, the Juggernauts would still be out
on the ice, down on their hands and knees, with thick marking
crayons such as the ones used to label timber in the woods, and
they would be marking crudely the hexagrammatics and baffling
limits and boundaries of their strange game. I have been to wrestling matches, since that time, and that is what the hang of air
was like, though the fans were quiet, and many wore ties, and sat
up straight, waiting: hands on their knees, even the women's legs
spread slightly apart, as if judging equipment at an auction, or
even animals. It was the way anything is, anything that is being
anticipated.

The games were sometimes violent, and always fast. We could
never get the hang of the rules, and for us the best part was before
the game, when the players crawled around on their knees with
their marking crayons, laboring to draw the colorful, crooked
lines, already suited up, and wearing the pads that would protect
them.

On a good night there would be maybe thirty-five fans: girlfriends, wives, and then too, the outcasts, spectators with nothing
else to do. There were people there who had probably driven from
Galveston, just for the nothing event. The few cars scattered
around in the huge parking lot outside nearly all had license plates
with different colors. Most of the players were from Pennsylvania
and New Jersey, and even beyond. It seemed odd to play the sport
in the springtime, as they did.

Everyone got their Cokes for free at the games. The players
didn't get any percentage of the gate, and they didn't even get
to play for free, but instead had to pay the Farmers' Market a

certain fee just to keep the lights on and the ice frozen; they paid
for that chance to keep playing a game that perhaps they should
have been slowing down in, or even stopping.

None of the Juggernauts wanted to stop! You could hear them
hitting the boards, the sides of the walls, when they slammed into
them. They skated so hard, and so fast! It was hypnotic, and you
felt you could watch it forever.

*E*d Odom drove a forest green Corvette to school, the old
kind from the sixties—older even than Kirby's—and he didn't
park in the faculty lot, but rather, on the other side of the con-
crete dividing posts, on the students' side, and he would arrive
early enough in the mornings—steamy already, the sun rising
above the apartment buildings and convenience stores, turning
the haze to a warm drip that had you sweating even before you
got to your locker—and he would cruise, so slowly, with the
windows down, one arm hanging out, around and around the
school, two times, three. Everyone saw him, and he saw everyone,
and would nod vaguely, a smile that looked just past and to the
side of a person, sliding away. He seemed to be like an athlete,
getting ready for an event.

In class, he would grow disdainful when the guys tried to ask
him about his "Vette:" what it would do, how long he had had
it, how much he had paid for it. He would look at some odd spot
in the room—a trash can, or the place in the corner where the
walls met the ceiling—and would seem disappointed in whom-
ever had asked the question, almost frozen with the disappoint-
ment, if not of that, then of something else—and he would seem
to be unable to move: pinned down by a thing. His head would
be cocked very slightly.

But one day he came to class looking like a thing from a
Halloween movie: all cut up and abraded, bruises the color of

melons and dark fruit, and a stupid expression on his normally wary face. His arm was in a sling. He looked as if the event had just happened, and he had come straight in off the street to find a phone. There was blood soaked through his gauze. The girls gasped. He looked straight at Laura DeCastagnola, who looked a little more shocked, and horrified, and also something else, than even the other girls—and even the guys, most of whom had no stuffing—even the guys looked away, and were queasy, could not look straight at him. Kirby and I watched the class, and it seemed only Laura was the one who could not take her eyes off him: one hand up to the side of her face, the way we all wanted to do, either in the dark or the light of day, while we whispered our promises eternal to her.

He sat down, slowly, without grimacing—focusing his mind somewhere else and far away to do so, it was easy to see—and we respected him forever, for that—and he opened the geometry book, and began to lecture.

Three days later, as the bruises began to wane, and he moved more easily, he finally told us—but our anticipation had long passed, after his initial refusal to tell us, back when it had first happened, and we had grown churlish and lost curiosity, and were merely disgusted at his childishness in holding the secret—all of us except Kirby and me, who were still hoping very much to find out. It was a thing that grew, in us, rather than fading away.

He had been driving down the highway, he said, and had opened the door to empty his litterbag—onto the highway!—and had leaned over too far, and had rolled out. His wife had been with him, and she had reached over with her long left leg and arm and drove, after he fell out.

"I bounced," he said, "like a basketball. While I was bouncing, and holding my ribs to keep them from breaking, I counted." He paused and looked intelligent, as if he had trapped us in a game of chess, but by now it was agreed upon, as if we had a pact, not to give him pleasure, and no one asked him, and he had to volunteer it.

"I bounced," he said clearly, enunciating quietly and with his teeth—it was like the words were an ice cream cone, and he was eating it slowly, on a hot day—"twenty-two times."

His wife, he said, drove to the next exit, went below the overpass, and came back and got him. Helped him back in the car.

We drove to the hockey games whenever we could. They didn't start until nine o'clock. Obviously all the players came home from work and ate supper first. The games lasted until eleven, twelve o'clock. There were fights among the fans sometimes, but rarely among the players, as in real hockey. I think that the fact they played among themselves, again and again, too many dulling intrasquad games, is what made this different. Though too it could just have been the spring. There weren't any wars, and there wasn't any racism, not in our lives, and we weren't hungry. There weren't any demands. Sometimes Kirby would pay for the tickets; sometimes I would.

Sometimes there would be a team not from our area, playing the Juggernauts: a northwest junior college's intramurals champions' team, or another, leaner and more haggard traveling band of ruffians, hangers-on in the sport: a prison team, sometimes, or worse. On these occasions the Juggernauts would rise from their rather smooth-skinned and sallow good-natured (though enthusiastic) boys'-school-type-of-play—happy, energetic zips of the skates, long gliding sweeps of mellowness on the ice, cradling the puck along and beaming—and on these invader nights, against the teams down from Connecticut, from Idaho, and Sioux Falls, they would turn fierce, like the same boys now squabbling over a favorite girl. On these nights of the visitors, the ticket prices rose to a dollar, and attendance would swell by half.

There would even be someone there with a camera and flash, a skinny youth but with a press card, perhaps real but probably manufactured, and good equipment, and he would be crouched low, moving around and around the rink like a spy, shooting pictures. And though there was no reason for a photographer to be there—the Juggernauts were in no league, none of these teams were, there was no official record of wins and losses—certainly no newspaper coverage—despite this, the Juggernauts always played hardest and wildest when the photographer was there. It could have been one of the players' sons or even grandsons, but that did not matter.

They skated with their bellies in, those nights, bumped into their opponents without apologies and knocked them to the ice (or were knocked to the ice themselves), and charged around on the ice with short savage chopping steps of their skate blades, as if trying in their anger to mince or hash the rink into a slush. Some of them would breathe through gritted teeth and shout, making low animal sounds.

The Juggernauts had a player we all called Larry Loop. He wasn't their captain, or anything—they were a band, not a team—and Larry Loop was large and chesty, and he raced down the ice in those crunching little high-knee steps whether they were playing against ax murderers or a seminarian's school. Friend or foe, Larry Loop would *run* on his skates rather than actually using them, and could travel just as fast that way, as it was the way he had taught himself to skate, and it was a thing to watch. You could tell he was not from the north. You could tell he had not grown up with the game, but had discovered it, late in life. He was big, and the oldest man on the ice, grey-headed, tufts of it sticking out from behind his savage, painted goalie's mask—

though he was not a goalie—and more often than not when he bumped into people, they went over.

It was amazing, actually, how easily the people Larry Loop crashed into went over when he hit them. They were just like something spilled. I think now that he had this great tactician's eye for analyzing, and would time his approach and hits—running at this odd, never-balanced velocity—so that he always made contact when they were pretty severely off-balance themselves: his victims nearly always seemed to be waving a leg high in the air, or grasping with both arms for useless sky, as they went over. And he would run a little farther, definitely pleased with himself, definitely smug, and then remember to turn back and look to see where the puck was, if it was still even in play.

He was called Larry Loop, we decided, because as he ran, he swung his stick, high and around, above his head, in a looping, whipping, exuberant circle, like a lariat, like a child pretending with one arm to be a helicopter. We almost expected to see him lift off. When you were close to it, you could hear the whistling sound it made.

He would gallop down the ice, waving his stick, drawing penalties for it the whole way, and I think it helped wind him up for the impact. He was what is called in hockey a "goon," an enforcer-type whose best contribution to the game is usually restricted to rattling the opposition's better players.

Except that pretty often Larry Loop would score goals, too. Again, perhaps, those strategian's eyes, theory and logic, because everything was all wrong, it shouldn't have been happening, he drew his stick back incorrectly and almost always shot improperly, off-balance. But one thing the thirty or so of us had learned from watching him was that when he was open and did shoot on goal, it was probably going to go all the way in.

When he scored, he went wild. He would throw his stick down onto the ice and race off in the opposite direction, in that funny little stamping run, and throw his masked face back, up at the low ceiling, and beat on his chest with his heavy gloved hands, and shout, "I am in LOVE! I am in LOVE!" It was funny, and it was frightening, too, to Kirby and me, like a visit to New York City for the first time, and we liked to believe that all the wildness and uncertainty and even danger in the world was contained there in that tiny skating rink, set so far out in the prairie, in the spring, heavy overhead blowers spinning, inside, to prevent the ice from melting. It was more ice than any of us had ever seen, that little arena, set so far out away from the rest of the town.

The wind coming across us, our faces, driving back into town— and it was town, then, and not yet city—it was as it had been on the way out to the game, only better, because there had been hope, going into the game, and it had not let us down. Larry Loop had been good and wild.

The rules were confusing, but we liked to watch. There wasn't any danger of, say, one of the players going down with an injury, while the rest of them crowded around him, until one of them looked up into the stands, directly at us, and motioned, or ordered, one of us to go down there and fill in: substitute. Those damn rules—not knowing what to do, and the panic such a thing would give us. It would be a horrible thing. We drove with the windows down, and felt as if we had escaped from something.

"When you are born," Big Ed said—and he turned and looked at the farthest side of the class and crouched, as if expecting an attack—there was maybe one small snicker, though by now, this late in the spring, most of the class was tired of his old grey-headed mock-youth—"the hospital, or wherever it is you were born, records the sound of your voice." He straightened up from his crouch and looked less wild, even calm.

"They record your first cries, the squawls you make when the doctor spanks you"—his eyes were looking at the floor, drifting everywhere but over Laura—"and they catalogue them with the FBI."

He was lecturing now, not story-telling. "Because every voice is like a set of fingerprints. They have special machines that separate and classify every broken-down aspect of your voice— and you can't disguise it, it's more unique than a set of finger-prints, it'll give you away quicker than anything, on a computer. Because those things in your voice that they pick up on tape don't ever change, over your life."

He seemed to take, for once, a pleasure in the actual content of this story, rather than in just the telling of it. Emily Carr, Laura's best friend but not a cheerleader, raised her hand and asked him—and she had a deep, husky, odd sort of voice, as if something was wrong with it, and was perhaps hoping it *would* change, with age—"What if you weren't born in a hospital? Or were born in a tiny little country hospital, where there wasn't even electricity, just a midwife?" Emily was from Oklahoma, and if possible, nicer even than Laura. Maybe because her voice was funny and off, but she went out of her way to smile at you, not afraid that you might get a crush on her, whereas Laura was shy and quick with her laughing monkey flash of white teeth, as if afraid she might lead you on into thinking something else. It was maybe like she already had someone. But it wasn't Ken! Ken was always running, running: sweating with the team. Scoring those goals.

"The FBI calls you," Big Ed said, with certainty. "If they don't have you on file, they just call you up, talk to you a while about some bogus sales offer—storm windows, insurance, Japanese Bi-bles—and then they hang up, and they've got you."

I dialed Kirby's number two days later, and didn't say anything when he answered.

"Hello?" he said, again. I hung up. But then the phone rang, and this time it was my turn to speak into the receiver, "Hello?," and not get an answer.

We practiced changing our voices, talked like ducks, like old men, like street toughs to each other, practicing for when the FBI called, and that moment was at hand. Tears of laughter rolled down our faces. We howled like hyenas. We could laugh at anything, and the pleasure of it was odd and sincere. Who would want to leave? If we couldn't date Laura and Emily, at least couldn't we be crazy, laughing all the time?

One Thursday night Kirby and I went out to the game, the Juggernauts were playing the team of an insurance firm from Boston that was in Houston for a convention—there were perhaps a hundred or more people in the stands, on either side of the teams—and we saw that number 52, wild Larry Loop, had his mask off for once, and he was talking to some people in the stands, only something was wrong, he wasn't really Larry Loop at all, it was Big Ed, Ed Adams, our geometry teacher, dressed up like Larry.

He looked like a clown, the clown that he was, standing there in the bulk of Larry's uniform, ice white and heavy rich blue: again, like a little boy, playing astronaut, playing hockey player. He was wearing Larry's big mittens and holding his stick, and hanging from his belt was the wild, frozen mask, a mute, noncommittal mouth cut into it for breathing. Big Ed was talking animatedly and, we could tell, intelligently, about the sport to a fan—a man in a business suit with a red tie and owl glasses, the tie swinging out away from him as he leaned against the glass to get closer to Larry Loop, to hear what he had to say.

We were howling again, at the audacity of Big Ed's trick at first, but even as we were registering that thought, we were taking note of the day he had come into class so battered, of the way he was now standing on the ice, in his skates, casually, and of how comfortable he appeared, talking, even while wearing the big suit.

We weren't even tempted to go down and meet him. Like quail in tall grass, we settled down deep into the back of the crowd and watched, without standing up, him play the whole game.

And the Juggernauts lost, twelve to eleven, though Big Ed, Larry, scored several goals, and we wanted to stay for the other part we liked, at the end, where the losing team—all sweaty and sore and exhausted—had to crawl around on the ice with rags, erasing the smeared and dulled blue and red stripes and boundary lines they had just put down hours before—they had to have it clean again, by morning, no signs that they had been out there and had had glory—and the Juggernauts, or whoever lost, would be crawling on the ice, wiping up the stripes, and grown men in hockey suits would be skating around with brooms, sweeping the ice smooth again—and it was a thing we liked to watch, and often did, but the crowd was gone this night, we were almost the only two left in there, and the arena wasn't the same any more, it was as threatening as a dark, slow lightning storm moving towards us, and we had to get out of there.

And walking out across the parking lot, trying to laugh and howl at the lunacy of it but also not able to—recognizing, and being troubled by, the first signs of insincerity in this paradox— we stopped, when we realized we were passing by a parked dark green Corvette, and that Laura was standing by it, and she was holding his coat and tie in her arms, the clothes he had worn in class that day, and she had the keys in her hand, and she wasn't a girl, she wasn't even Laura, she was just some woman standing there, waiting for her man, with hopes and fears and other thoughts on her mind, a thousand other thoughts, she was just living, and it wasn't pretend.

The night was dark, without a moon, and she held our surprised looks, and in two months she would be graduating, and what she was doing would be okay then, we suddenly realized, if it was ever okay, and for the first time we saw the thing, in its immensity, and it was like coming around a bend or a trail in the woods and suddenly seeing the hugeness and emptiness of a great plowed pasture or field, when all one's life up to that point has been spent close to but never seeing a field of that size. It was so large that it was very clear to us that the whole rest of our lives would be spent in a field like that, crossing it, and the look Laura gave us was sweet and kind, but also wise, and was like an old familiar welcome.

This was back in those first days when Houston was clean and just growing, not yet beginning to die or get old. Houston was young, then, too. You cannot imagine how smooth life was for you, if you were in high school, that one spring, when oil was $42 a barrel, and everyone's father was employed by the petroleum industry, and a hero for finding oil when the Arabs wouldn't sell us any. Anything was possible.

MISSISSIPPI

～

As you know, there are no more Coca-Colas in Mississippi. There aren't any cokes anywhere. They changed them; they did away with them, the fuckers. Except at my farmhouse. I have approximately two thousand seven hundred and forty-four of them in those little wooden flats that they used to ship them around in, faded, red and historic.

When I have a bad day at work I will go home and throw three or four of them against the rocks in the back pasture.

I have never been married but a fat rich girl asked me once. And this: this! People who borrow books, and then don't return them! Obscenity! These people are scum and vermin, and the stuff that rolls around in balls and lurks in the corners on the wood floor beneath your high bed in the guest room: crash, crash, crash! There go three more Cokes for the morons and diarrhea people who do not return books but treat them instead as decks of cards, pencils, chewing gum. Oh may I borrow a piece of paper? And then they never return them.

The fat girl who asked me to marry her bought me all those Cokes before leaving, and also said, oftentimes, that love was just saying ah what the heck and letting go, and accepting. She said that, yes: that love was accepting. And then she went out and bought about three hundred years' worth of Cokes, because she didn't like the new formula.

Mosquitoes would feast on us when we slept on the bed by the open window, even though there was a screen. She drank a lot of Cokes. And her dog had fleas! The little pooch would stay over when she did, slept at the foot of the bed. The big rich girl's name was Leanne. Take off the last two letters and she was lean. She had the kiss of an angel, though. When she kissed you it was like going swimming in the ocean on a hot day with a bunch of people standing around applauding. And I loved her.

*T*here are all these feral hounds in the woods where I live. And when we made love they would all start howling. I don't know if it was coincidence or not. We usually made love about the same time every night. Pretty much the same way. None of this has anything to do with how sweet and truly good she was.

*H*er father was in oil, oil was in her father. He used to say: "Finding oil is not so complex. It is really nothing more than deciding what you like. Everyone, all geologists, have access to pretty much the same set of facts. You just have to decide which ones you like in order to get to what it is you are looking for."

He was a mystic. But he voted for Republicans! They took less of his money, he said. They left more of it for him to spend on his daughter and mean son, he said.

And his son *was* mean. His name was Hector. When he was a child if he didn't like the clothes his oil father had put out for him to wear to school the next day, he would begin setting fire to things. I grew up with him. An absolute rotgut devil! He was as handsome as Leanne was fat. He would grow a moustache and then steal the girlfriends from people he didn't like or who had crossed him. Just for a day, or a week.

And he was in fights. And he drove fast. Yet we would go fishing together and he would be very gentle in taking the fish off the hook, wet his hands first before handling it, etc. The breezes came under our arms and around us. Dragonflies would dab the water with their stingers. He liked me basically because I liked (loved) Leanne, and as I said before, she was wonderful. We both knew that. We would be sitting there together on a log on a clay bank, and he would know that I thought she was wonderful.

She could make you cry, just watching her, when the wind was in her hair. She could stand over the big river in New Orleans, or outside on the back porch, or even in town, shopping, and you'd love her. She would always have something in her purse for me, and never mind what Hector and I did to the cars and sometimes the arms and legs of anyone who laughed at her. Because of her bigness. Because of their smallness.

I'm pretty plump myself. I'm short. I have a temper. My nose is big and long. If I drink coffee it smells like death and end-of-world when I go to the bathroom and make big dirt. Leanne and her brother and I were going to drill for oil on the farm I rent. It is in Russum, Mississippi, in the wild big fairway of pumping and producing oil wells coming up from Louisiana and through Natchez that is said to end a good many miles south of Russum but they are wrong. After we found the oil, Hector was going to go to Montana and live like a jerk-off in a cabin with nothing to do but fish and drink and be happy all day. His father wouldn't give him any money to leave the state with because he knew Hector would be gone if he did. Leanne was going to use the money to get skinny. I was going to go to school. I was going to get educated and learn things. It would be a dream well. Everything would be solved.

"I know there's oil under this fucking farm," Hector would say. He would stamp his feet and stomp all around, as if daring it to come up or something, like a gopher. We believed him. Hector was like magic when he was angry.

Summers in Mississippi are like this: no one else exists in the world. They're that good. You can hang your cotton sheets on the line and the sun in them that night as you lie on them will make you have erections all night long. Our crickets are trained to sing prettier and more convincing and purely than nature should allow. Mississippi is a special place. Some days I like to go out in the tall grass and roll around like a dog.

The Auto-View Drive-In Theatre in Port Gibson, Mississippi, on the river, is only forty minutes away, and the moon will come up full and delightful behind the screen, like a grinning thing, on the last Saturday of the month. I don't know if they built the theatre that way or if the moon chose that place and seeks it out. These are little things but even so you can count on them, and others, daily. I lived in Chicago once and when I have nightmares occasionally it is to there that I return. There is a tremendous amount of love to be had in the numerous small things, and I think happiness is chiefly the adding up of a whole lot of little passions until a snowball effect is created and you find yourself playing in the midst of the big passions, love and hate, and running down the road and loving everything, consuming, consuming. Coca-Colas and mailboxes and fat girls and their dogs. I like the state of Mississippi. You can hear bull frogs down on the creek out the window at night.

Water beetles! Water Beetles! We have water beetles, and they smell like roses! She showed them to me. We were driving around in her old car with the flea-dog and lots of money for lunch, and she stopped by a pond and showed me how to wade out and gather these little shelled diving bugs that smelled remarkably like roses.

Once Hector and I caught an alligator snapping turtle. It weighed a hundred and fifty pounds. We were fishing with cane poles. Worms. His pole bent, and then snapped. The lost half of the pole sailed out into the creek. Hector said shit, angrily, and dived in after it. The turtle was already headed back down to bury in the mud. You can never get them out once they have buried themselves like that. Hector grabbed the line (35-pound mono: heavy enough to cut your hand like a laser, if you pull too hard) and began twanging it like a guitar string. He was saying shit and damn and calling the turtle a fucker. The vibrations on the line made the worm in the turtle's mouth feel like an operating car wash and made him not want to burrow in the mud.

"Fucker! Shit-brown! Ass goober!" Hector cried. He was in the shallows now on the other side of the creek and was dragging the thrashing reptile into the shallows too. I was twenty-five. The air smelled like hay and yellow flowers. Leanne would have had fun seeing the turtle. He got burrowed in the mud while Hector was trying to pull him out. Hector called me to wade in and help pull on his tail but we could not budge him. He made me stand there and hold that turtle by the tail on this hot day while he went to get the jeep. We got the fucker.

The farmhouse I rent now is only three miles from this place where we used to fish. That is what my state is about. You know what I mean. I can go out on the porch in the morning and don't have to bother remembering things because nothing is forgotten.

Sometimes the air is purple, and smells of tornadoes, but it is all the same, if you haven't forgotten.

*O*wls. We got owls. At night they say whoo, and make you question your place in things, and even sometimes what is in you.

*H*ector let the turtle snap up a piece of pine log and with his mouth thus occupied we took turns sitting on his back riding around on him. I thought it would be fun to take him to the town and show him off along with our muscles, but Hector said no, there were fuckers there in town and they would poke sticks at him. We fed the turtle a road map, a tennis ball, two apples and a warm tunafish sandwich, and then let him go.

"Goodbye, you fucker," Hector cried after him. The turtle was red-eyed and running for the creek like some kind of athlete. Hector shook his fist at the turtle. He was truly happy. "Goodbye, you fucker!" he cried again. There was triumph and victory and key elements of the Magna Charta in his voice; for the rest of the week Hector was like flowing water when he smiled.

Listen, my state is this, too: the girls have pretty bosoms, under their swim suits. (Biloxi). The yellow dresses that they wear over bare ankles make you shiver when the wind blows.

"*A*nger is as good as love," Hector would say, more than once and in various ways. "I love feeling things. I am not afraid to feel the bad passions as well as the good. As long as I do not hurt anyone, sometimes I really love getting good and angry. I think the important thing is to not forget anything: to feel all passions and always be aware of them."

God, he was angry. We would eat peaches there on the creek

and they would taste like August. The fences around the meadows were rusted and made of barbed wire. I would take naps now, though we didn't then, and I haven't forgotten anything. There were hawks that flew overhead.

They say as you get older you tend to be more mellow, not so angry, but with Hector's help, I am learning. Always she was doing things like that: buying me Cokes, borrowing my car and putting new tires on it, or subscribing to a magazine for me. And I forgot: I took these things for granted, let them slip away, so that now I am having to try hard to remember them. I am nothing, compared to Hector. If Hector knew I had those Cokes he would flush them down the toilet. He would swing baseball bats at them. He would think about people who judged you by looks or money and he would quite possibly drive his jeep through the living room and into the den, where most of those bottles are stacked.

We go way back, Hector and me.

We worked together for a moving company once, with a boss who had a face like a grin-baring vampire and who overworked us while still smiling. Hector threw a pie in his face and then asked for a raise.

You can cheat the phone company out of twenty-five cents, too. You call them up and tell them you lost a quarter in a pay phone at so-and-so location. They will send you a check for twenty-five cents, or credit your account. Hector showed me this. Hector would do it dozens of times each month.

There are wild turkeys in the woods. When it rains it smells like orchids out here. None of the preachers have any spit or love to them but they can be avoided. Tornadoes are exciting. They said the governor was a homosexual but he got elected anyway. When you are canoeing at night and the paddle first goes into the water it sounds like God is talking to you.

Drill for oil; eat seafood, wiping its salty goodness from your dripping mouth onto the tablecloth or napkin. Fish for flounder;

catch monster turtles in the creeks. Oh, sir, I love my state! Passion, passion, lust! Hector's father once told Hector and me that when he drilled for oil he imagined he was lowering his own penis into the earth, hot and seeking, searching for the oil. They say Hector's mother was beautiful.

*L*eanne got mad and went away when I said I didn't want to marry her. She went to California and I suppose she has lost a lot of weight and changed her hair and is spending money. She can come back if she wants but it won't be the same. She will have forgotten.

Hector and I still go fishing. We talk about the oil well we are going to drill. We drink Cokes. We will not change. Hector is still angry. I still love Leanne. If she comes back and asks me again this time I will marry her. I have learned, from the people in my state, and that is what my answer will be.

IN RUTH'S COUNTRY

The rules for dating Mormon girls were simple.

No coffee; no long hair.

No curse words; one kiss.

That was about it. It was simple. Anyone could do it.

Utah is an odd state—the most beautiful, I think—because it is one thing but also another. It is red and hot in the desert—in the south—while the north has the cool and blue forests and mountains, which smell of fir and snow. And like so many things, when seen from a distance, they look unattainable, like a mystery, or a promise.

My uncle and I were not Mormons. We lived in southern Utah, Uncle Mike and I and the rest of the town of Moab. In the summers, at night, thunderstorms would sometimes roll across the dry valley, illuminating the cliffs with flashes of lightning. There would be the explosions of light and for a second—beneath the cliffs—we could see the dry creeks and the town itself. The town had wide streets, like a stagecoach town in a Hollywood prop.

There would be flash floods out in the desert: water so muddy and frothy, churning, that its anger was almost obscene, and it was anger. But then the floods were gone quickly, and they were easy to avoid in the first place, if you knew about them and knew to stay out of their way, even out of the places where they could occur.

Tourists moved through our town on their way to the national parks. They reminded me of the bloated steers I would sometimes see floating down the Colorado, sweeping along with the current. The steers I saw were the ones that had fallen over the steep cliffs and into the river below; but the tourists came only in the summers.

Mormons couldn't date non-Mormons. It was a logical rule. There were different values, or so it was supposed, so we chose to believe.

Among the elders of Moab there were corny handshakes, secret meeting rooms, silly passwords, but because I was young, I could move through the town and among the people. I could observe, as long as I made no threats against the religion's integrity, no overtures against its gene pool.

I was allowed to watch.

There was a Mormon girl, Ruth, whom I wanted to get to know. She was two years younger than I was, but I liked the way she watched things. She looked at the tourists, and it seemed to me that she too might have been thinking about the cows, the ones that sometimes went over the cliffs. She looked at the sky sometimes, checking for I don't know what.

Other times I would see her watching me. I liked it, but knew better than to like it too much. I tried not to like it, and I tried not to watch back.

It did cross my mind, too, that perhaps she was just crazy, slightly retarded, to be looking at me for so long, so directly. Just watching.

That was how different things were. I really did not believe she could just be watching, and thinking.

*U*ncle Mike and I ran wild cattle in the sage for a living, scrub steers that could handle the heat and rattlesnakes and snows of winter. The country in which the cattle were turned out was too vast for fences. Instead, we used brands, or nothing.

Sometimes the cattle would be down along a salt creek in a willow flat, grazing in the dry field behind an old beaver dam. Other times they would be back up in the mesas and plateaus, hiding in the rocks.

They had all the country they wanted, and their movements seemed to be mostly whimsical. All of the cattle were about the same size, and sometimes, in trying to cut yours away from the others, out of the big herd for market—for slaughter—if you got someone else's cow, it was all right to go ahead and take that one instead of the one you wanted. They were all pretty much the same.

But if you had scruples, you had to tell the person whose cow it was, when you did that, so that he could take one of yours.

It wasn't a thing Uncle Mike and I ever worried about, because we were good at cutting the cattle, and we hardly ever picked out anyone else's cattle, even by mistake. We knew what we were doing, and as long as we didn't make mistakes—if the job was done properly—there wasn't a need for rules, scruples, or morals in the first place.

What you had to remember about cutting cattle—and it was a thing Uncle Mike had told me—was to pretend that you were capable of being in two places at once: where the cow was going; and where it wanted to go.

You had to get there ahead of it.

We cut them on foot with our barking dogs. Sometimes we'd use the jeep. It was hard work, and it seemed to need doing constantly. Without fences, the cattle were always trying to drift north. The blue mountains shimmered, and seemed a place to go to. The mountains looked cooler than anything we had ever seen.

So I couldn't ask Ruth out. And why would I want to? One lousy kiss? She was flatchested, like a seven-year old boy, and she wore librarian's gold wire-rimmed glasses, grandmother glasses.

Her hair was a reddish color—the kind that you think is brown until it gets out into the sun—and it was thick. I was slightly jealous of all her freckles, and also of the old overalls she was always wearing. They looked as if they made her feel good, because she was always smiling, even if only slightly. I imagined what the denim softness felt like, on her ankles, on her thighs, and going higher.

*I*t was good, being out on the north end of town the way we were. At seventeen and eighteen, one expects the things that happen, I think; they do not come as a surprise, no matter what. Sometimes Mike and I would sit out on the patio and drink a beer or some vodka, or gin-and-tonics, with ice and limes—limes from faraway, tropical cultures—and we would watch the purple part of dusk rising up out of the dry valley, moving toward us, covering the desert like a spill. And the lights in town below would come on, in the purple valley.

Ruth's old Volkswagen came up our long road one evening, trailing dust from a long way off, and when she pulled up and got out she did not hesitate, but walked up to Uncle Mike and said that her car was dying on cool mornings, and also on hills, and that she needed new windshield wipers too.

It was frightening, her having come up out of the valley like that and into our part of the desert, driving in such a straight line to get there. She just did it. But once she was there, I did not want her to leave. I knew it did not fit with the unspoken deal Mike and I had cut with the town, but I liked her being up there, on our plateau, and wasn't eager for her to go back down.

"This is a beautiful view," she said, looking around at the

purple dusk and the lights coming on in town. I offered her my drink, which I had not tasted yet, and she sipped it, not even knowing what it was. Mike went in the garage to look at her car. I got a chair for Ruth and seated her. We didn't say anything, just watched the desert, until it was completely dark.

After a while, Mike came out of the garage with her old spark plugs, but I knew that spark plugs wouldn't make her car do what it was she said it was doing.

"Your wipers look fine," he said. "The spark plugs will be five dollars."

She took the money from her shirt pocket—some of it in bills, some in coins—and she handed it to him.

We sat there and each had another drink, and then the wind started to blow, the way it did every night, and made the wind chimes tinkle back in the garage.

There was lightning to the south. We saw it almost every night, but it never seemed to reach Moab. Then, going home, driving back to town: her brake lights, tiny and red.

*T*here was one man, a bishop in the church, the head bishop for all of Moab—his name was Homer—and he was an attorney, the richest man in town. He had thousands of cattle, maybe more than anyone in Utah. The way he got his cattle when he wanted them for market was to send some of his men out into the desert with rifles to shoot them.

It was lazy and simple and I thought it was wrong. The men would load the dead cattle into their trucks that way, and take them to Bishop Homer's own slaughterhouse. We had to bring ours in alive.

Uncle Mike and I did not like Bishop Homer, but we did not waste time worrying about him either.

It was my job to keep Uncle Mike's and my cattle away from the others, if I could. Every day after school, Ruth and I drove out into the desert in the jeep all that spring, and we chased Bishop Homer's cattle with the dogs. We tried to keep his red-eyed, wormy dwarves away from our registered Hereford heifers. Bishop Homer had his men buy whatever passed through the auction circle at a low price, whether it was healthy or not—he didn't look at the quality of an animal at all—and we tried to cut Mike's and my cattle out of the big herds, and to keep them by themselves. All of the cattle gathered at the rim of the gorge, high up over the river, and they were always trying to find different trails leading down. There wasn't any way to get to the river—the cliffs were basalt, straight up and down—but the cattle watched the river daily, as if expecting that a new path might miraculously appear.

The bulls were always hopping up on our heifers. Bishop Homer had it in his mind that the bulls could survive the desert better than the heifers, and he was particularly keen to buy any bulls that passed through the auction, no matter that he already had too many. He was too lazy to have them turned into steers. He just turned them out.

The dogs raced alongside the stampeding bulls, snapping and barking. We ran along and behind them, shouting and throwing rocks, whenever we found them in with our heifers. Their great testicles tangled between their legs when they tried to run too fast, and were an easy target. It was a hot spring, and Bishop Homer's cattle began to lose weight.

Ruth and I made picnics. We carried mayonnaise jars wrapped in newspaper to keep them cool, full of lemonade with ice cubes rattling, and we took a blanket. There were sandbars down in the river gorge, and some days we would climb down the dangerous cliffs to them. There were caves along the river, dark recesses out of which small birds flew, back and forth into the sunlight. The water was cold and green and moving very fast.

"Can you swim?" Ruth asked one day.

"Yes," I told her, though I could not, and was hoping she would not ask me to show her. I would have had to try, and almost certainly would have drowned.

"I don't know if I can or not," she said. She didn't seem particularly frightened, however.

Other days we talked about Bishop Homer as we chased his cattle. He was in charge of Ruth's ward. That was a church subdivision, like a platoon or a brigade.

Ruth had taken an after-school job that spring as Bishop Homer's secretary. He was good friends with her parents, and it was how she got the job.

"He's got three wives," she said. "The one here in town, plus one in St. George, and one up north, in Logan."

Logan was a ski town, in the very northern part of the state. It took a lot of money to live in Logan, and it was usually where the not-so-very-good Mormons went, because it was a good place to have fun. A lot of people in Moab looked at Logan wistfully, on the map. I wondered what the wife in Logan was like.

The bulls ran ahead of us at a steady trot, a sort of controlled panic; sometimes they stumbled but caught themselves.

"I'm not supposed to know that," Ruth shouted. "I'm the only one who knows."

We stopped the jeep and watched the cattle on the trail ahead, still trotting, back up into the rocks, to where there was no grass or water, not even a thin salt creek. I thought about how far we were from anything.

There was a hawk out over the gorge, doing slow circles, and Ruth told me that Bishop Homer had touched her once.

The engine was baking in the heat, making ticks and moans, and the wind was gusting, lifting the jeep off its shocks and rocking it. We watched the hawk and were pleased when we saw it fold its wings and dive, with a shrill cry, into the gorge.

Later in the spring our heifers began dropping more calves. Wildflowers and cactus blossoms were everywhere. There were dwarf calves, red calves, ugly cream-colored calves, and stillborns. They all had to be taken away to market; not a one was worth keeping.

Mike and I had Ruth over for dinner. She had church meetings almost every day, but she skipped some of them. We drank the gin-and-tonics, and it was okay for her to sit with her head in my lap, or mine in hers. The wind on the back patio was better than it had ever been that year; it seemed to bring new scents from new places, and it was stronger. Sometimes Ruth asked me if I was afraid of dying.

We didn't associate much in school. Being younger, she wasn't in any of my classes, and it would have been trouble for her to be seen with me too often. Her parents didn't like her spending the evenings out on my porch, but she told them she was proselytizing. So it was all right, and she kept coming out to our place to sit up there in the evenings.

And then it was summer. We had more time than we could ever have wished for.

We had all the time anyone could ever need, for anything.

*O*ur heifers were still dropping ruinous calves, and Mike said it had to stop. So one day, knowing what we were doing, and with the dogs to help us, we ran three of Bishop Homer's woolly bulls right over the gorge, and we shouted, throwing things, and chased them toward it. Their fear took care of the rest.

We stood there, slightly dizzy, exultant, and looked at the green river below, the slow-moving spills of white that we knew were rapids. One of the bulls was broken on the rocks and two were washing through the rapids.

"How many cattle would you say he has?" Ruth asked me. She slipped her hand in mine.

I didn't know.

"What are his other two wives' names?" I asked her. She had told me Bishop Homer was still bothering her.

We watched that hawk again—it seemed to have come from nowhere, right in front of us, I could see the light brown and cream of its breast—and Ruth told me that their names were Rebecca and Rachel.

"You're going to stay with your Uncle Mike and work on trucks and cars, and raise the wild cattle, too, aren't you, is that right?" she asked, on our way back. It was dark by then, with bright stars and the night winds starting up. The stars seemed to glimmer and flash above us, we didn't have a top on the jeep, and instead of lying to her, I told her yes, it was what I would continue to do.

We stopped wearing clothes when we were out in the desert in July, hot July: just our tennis shoes and socks. We raced the jeep, wearing our seat belts, and we set up small piles of stones, up high on the slickrock domes, where we could see forever, and we practiced racing around them, and cornering: we designed intricate, elaborate courses, through which we tried to race at the fastest possible speed.

She was starting, finally, to get her breasts, which was all right with me. Both of us were lean, from chasing the bulls. The sun felt good, on our backs, our legs. We drove fast, wearing nothing.

A bad thing was happening with the cattle, however; with Bishop Homer's cattle. They were getting used to being chased, and would not run so far, or so easily; sometimes we had to ram them with the jeep to get them even to break into a grudging trot.

The desert was like a park that summer. Flowers bloomed as never before: a different batch, different colors, every couple of weeks. It stormed almost every night, the heat of the day building up and then cooling quickly. The lightning storms rocketed up and down the cliffs of the river, and into town.

Sometimes we made it back to Mike's in time to watch the purple and then the darkness as it sank over the desert, like stage lighting, like the end of a show. But we didn't always make it, and then we would watch from one of the slickrock domes, or we would hike up and sit beneath one of the eerie, looping rock arches.

Some nights there was an early moon, and we could see the cattle, grazing on the worthless sage, and the jackrabbits moving around, too, everything ghostly in that light, everything coming out after dark.

But other nights the storms would wash through quickly, windy drenching downpours that soaked us, and it was fun to sit on the rocks and let the storm hit us and beat against us. The nights were always warm, though cooler after those rains, and the smells were so sharp as to make us imagine that something new was out there, something happening that had never happened to anyone before.

It was a good summer. Though there were too many cattle and too much grazing on the already spare land, the cattle did not eat the bitter flowers, and as a result, wild blooming blue and yellow weeds and wine-colored cactus blossoms rushed into the spots where the weak grasses had been, sprouting up out of the dried cattle droppings.

In August, the mountains to the north took on a darker blue. And the smells seemed to change. They were coming from another direction. From behind us, from the north.

Occasionally, Ruth's parents would ask her how I was doing, if I was thinking about changing yet. "Converting," was the term they used; and even the thought of it terrified me.

Ruth said that she had told them I was very close: very, very close.

She watched me as she said this. We were sitting on the boulders down by the white rapids, throwing driftwood branches into the center.

Then, up above us, I saw a man looking down, a man with a camera. He was up on the rim. He was so far up there. He took pictures of us while we sat on the rocks, and I looked up at him but didn't move, because there was not much I could do; our clothes were up by the jeep. Ruth didn't see him, and I didn't want to alarm her. Just a lost tourist, I thought. A lost tourist with a big lens.

But it was him, of course. I found that out soon enough, though I didn't know what he looked like. When we got back up on the rim, I saw his cattle company's pale blue truck, tiny and raising dust, moving slowly away to the north, and I realized that he had come into the desert for some of his cows.

Ruth didn't say much all the rest of the day, but that evening, driving home, when we stopped at a junkyard outside the city limits and pulled in and turned the lights off, she looked at all the old rusting heaps and goggle-eyed wrecks, and then, as if we had been married for fifteen years, she helped me get the picnic blanket out. The night was warm and we lay there among the wrecks, and I thought that one of us would get her soul, Homer or myself, and wasn't sure I wanted it. It seemed like a pretty big thing to take, even if she was determined to be rid of it.

We were home before midnight, as was the rule.

We did other new things, too, after that. Some new ground was opened up, it seemed, and we had more space in which to move, more things to see and look at and study. We learned how to track Gila monsters in the sand. Their heavy tails dragged behind them like clubs and they rested in the shade of the sagebrush. We would patiently track them, in our tennis shoes, following their staggering trail from shade bush to shade bush. Eventually, we would catch up with them.

They would be orange and black, beaded, motionless, and we never got too close to them once we had found them. The most beautiful thing in the desert was also the most dangerous.

We had a rule of our own. Any time we found a Gila monster, we had to kiss: slowly, and with everything we had.

We waded in the river, too, above the rapids. I was still afraid to go out into the deep and attempt swimming. But it was a game to see how close we could get to the rapids' pull. Knee-deep, for Ruth; her small behind, like a fruit, as she stood in the current, and felt the water shuddering against her legs, the backs of her knees.

Down in the gorge like that, there was only sun, and river, and sky, and the boulders around which the river flowed. I watched for the man with the camera, but he did not come back. Ankle-deep, and then knee-deep, I would come up behind Ruth, hold her hand, and then go out a little farther. The water beat against my thighs, splashing and spraying against me. She didn't try to pull me back. She thought it was fun. And it was; but I kept expecting her to tighten her grip, and try to pull me back into the shallows.

Her hair was getting longer, more bleached, and she was just watching, laughing, holding her hand out at full arm's length for me to hold on to. But she would have let go if I had slipped and gone down.

As the summer moved on, the thunderstorms that had been building after dusk were fewer and smaller; mostly it was just dry wind. Ruth had missed her period, and though I was troubled for her, worrying about her church and her parents' reaction, I didn't mind at all, not a bit. In fact, I liked it. I put my hand on it all the time, which pleased her.

But I knew that, unlike me, she had to be thinking of other things.

We still chased the cattle. Once in the jeep we ran an old stud Brangus over the edge, and got too close. A sliding swerve, gravel under our tires; we hit a rock and went up on two wheels and almost went over. All the way down.

I had names picked out. I was going to build my own house, out even farther north, away from town, away from everything, and Ruth and I would be just fine. I had names picked out, if it was a boy.

I was picturing what life would be like, and it seemed to me that it could keep on being the same. I could see it as clearly as I thought I'd ever seen anything.

I thought because she liked the gin-and-tonics, and the river wading, and chasing cows, Ruth would change. Convert. I knew she liked her church, believed in it, attended it, but I took for granted that as she grew larger, she would not remain in it, and she would come out a little north of town to live with me. That was the picture. In my mind, the picture became the truth, and I didn't worry about anything.

Tumbleweeds blew down the center of Main Street, late at night. Dry and empty, they rolled like speedballs, hopping and skipping, smashing off the sides of buildings. They rolled like an army through town. We would sit on the sidewalk sometimes and wait for them, looking down the street—the town like a ghost town, that late at night—the wind would be in our faces, and we could never hear the tumbleweeds coming, but could only watch, and wait.

Then, finally, very close to ten o'clock, their dim shapes would come blowing toward us from out of the darkness. We would jump up and run out into their midst, and, as if they were medicine balls, we would try to catch them.

They weighed nothing. We would turn and try to run along with them, running down the center of Main Street, heading south and out of town, but we could never keep up, and we would have to stop for breath somewhere around Parkinson's Drug Store. Mike had said that tumbleweeds were more like people than anything else in the world; that they always took the easiest path—always—and that the only way they would stop was if something latched on to them, or trapped them. A branch, a rock, a dead-end alley. . . .

During the last week in August, the north winds began to grow cool, and we wore light sweaters on the back porch. Ruth sipped her drink and kept one of her Mormon bibles—they had five or six—in her lap, and sometimes browsed through it. She'd never carried it around like that, and I found it slightly disturbing, but there were new smells, fresher and sharper, coming from the north, and sometimes we would turn and look back in that direction, though it would be dark and we would see nothing.

But we could imagine.

The winds made the mountains smell as beautiful as they must have looked.

Neither of us had ever been up in the mountains, but we had the little things, like the smells in the wind, that told us they were there, and even what they were like. Sometimes Ruth turned her head all the way around so that the wind was directly in her face, blowing her hair back.

She would sip her drink. She would squint beneath the patio light, and read.

It was a cold wind.

I had told Mike about Ruth and he had just nodded. He hadn't said anything, but I felt as if he was somehow pleased; it seemed somehow, by the way he worked in the garage, to be a thing he was looking forward to seeing happen. I know that I was.

I rolled the jeep one day in August—no heat out in the desert, just a mild shimmering day, we were clothed—and I don't remember how I did it, exactly. There weren't any cattle around, but we were driving fast, just to feel the wind. Sometimes, over rises, the jeep would leave the ground, flying, and then it would come down with a smash, shaking the frame. We went over one rise, I think, and must have gotten too high, and came down on our side, Ruth's side.

When we came to a stop, we were hanging upside down, saved by our belts, with broken glass all in our hair and the radiator steaming and tires hissing, and all sorts of fluids—strong-smelling gasoline, water, oils—dripping on us as if in a light rain. There was a lot of blood, from where Ruth's leg had scraped across the rocks, skidding beneath the jeep, and I shouted her name, because she wasn't moving.

I still remember the way I screamed for her. Sometimes I think it would be possible to still go out into that part of the desert and hunt the scream down, like some wild animal, track it right up into a canyon, and find it, still bouncing around off the rocks, never stopping—the sound waves still going—Ruth's name, shouted by me, as she hung upside down, swinging, arms hanging, hair swinging, glasses hanging from one ear, everything all wrong, everything all pointed the wrong way.

Mike came in his station wagon and found us with a search-light, when we did not get in that night.

What Ruth did next was very strange. About two weeks later she stopped seeing me. I went to Bishop Homer's law office where she was working full time, and I asked to see her.

She came out into the hall, looking very different, very changed. She had on a new dress and she was holding one of the bibles against her chest, almost clutching it. She seemed somehow frightened of me, but also almost disdainful.

"Ruth," I said, and looked at her. She was all dressed up, and wouldn't say anything. She was just looking at me: that look as if she was afraid I wanted to take something from her, that look that said, too, that she could kill me if I tried.

"The baby, Ruth," I said. I ran a hand through my hair. I was wearing my old cattle-chasing clothes, and I felt like a boy, out there in the hall. There was no one else around. We were in a strange building, a strange hallway, and the river seemed very far away.

"Not yours," she said suddenly. She clutched the Bible even tighter. There were tears in her eyes. "Not yours," she said again. It's the thing I think of most, when I think about it now, how hard it probably was for her to say that.

She sent the pictures and the negatives to me after she was settled in the mountains, in a town called Brigham City. It was about three hundred miles to the north.

Uncle Mike and I still cut our cattle for market. Bishop Homer still sends his men out into the desert to shoot his. Some days I still sit up in the rocks, with the old dogs and the jeep, and try to ambush his sorry bulls and chase them over the cliff; but other days, I just sit there and listen to the silence.

Sometimes the dogs and I go swimming in the water above the rapids.

I try to imagine myself as being two people, in two places at once, but I cannot do it, not as well as I used to be able to.

Mike and I work on the trucks and cars together now. I hold the light for him, peering up into the dark maw of the engine, trying to see what part has gone wrong, what part is missing. It is hard work and sometimes we make the wrong choices.

One of us was frightened, too frightened, and though I've thought about it ever since, I still can't figure out which of us it was.

I wonder how she is. I wonder what the things are that frighten her most now.

WILD HORSES

~~

*K*aren was twenty-six. She had been engaged twice, married once. Her husband had run away with another woman after only six months. It still made her angry when she thought about it, which was not often.

The second man she had loved more, the most. He was the one she had been engaged to, but had not married. His name was Henry. He had drowned in the Mississippi the day before they were to be married. They never even found the body. He had a marker in the cemetery, but it was a sham. All her life, Karen had heard those stories about fiancés dying the day before the wedding; and then it had happened to her.

Henry and some of his friends, including his best friend, Sydney Bean, had been sitting up on the old railroad trestle, the old highway that ran so far and across that river, above the wide muddiness. Louisiana and trees on one side; Mississippi and trees, and some farms, on the other side—the place from which they had come. There had been a full moon and no wind, and they had been sitting above the water, maybe a hundred feet above it, laughing, and drinking Psychos from the Daquiri World over in Delta, Louisiana. The Psychos contained rum and Coca-Cola and various fruit juices and blue food coloring. They came in styro-

1 4 7

foam cups the size of small trash cans, so large they had to be held with both hands. They had had too many of them: two, maybe three apiece.

Henry had stood up, beaten his chest like Tarzan, shouted, and then dived in. It had taken him forever, just to hit the water; the light from the moon was good, and they had been able to watch him, all the way down.

Sometimes Sydney Bean still came by to visit Karen. Sydney was gentle and sad, her own age, and he worked somewhere on a farm, out past Utica, back to the east, where he broke and sometimes trained horses.

Once a month—at the end of each month—Sydney would stay over on Karen's farm, and they would go into her big empty closet, and he would let her hit him: striking him with her fists, kicking him, kneeing him, slapping his face until his ears rang and his nose bled; slapping and swinging at him until she was crying and her hair was wild and in her eyes, and the palms of her hands hurt too much to hit him any more.

It built up, the ache and the anger in Karen; and then, hitting Sydney, it went away for a while. He was a good friend. But the trouble was that it always came back.

Sometimes Sydney would try to help her in other ways. He would tell her that some day she was going to have to realize that Henry would not be coming back. Not ever—not in any form— but to remember what she had had, to keep *that* from going away.

Sydney would stand there, in the closet, and let her strike him. But the rules were strict: she had to keep her mouth closed. He would not let her call him names while she was hitting him.

Though she wanted to.

After it was over, and she was crying, more drained than she had felt since the last time, sobbing, her feelings laid bare, Sydney would help her up. He would take her into the bedroom and towel her forehead with a cool washcloth. Karen would be crying in a child's gulping sobs, and he would brush her hair, hold her hand, even hold her against him, and pat her back while she moaned.

Farm sounds would come from the field, and when she looked out the window, she might see her neighbor, old Dr. Lynly, the vet, driving along in his ancient blue truck, moving along the bayou, down along the trees, with his dog, Buster, running alongside, barking; herding the cows together for vaccinations.

"I can still feel the hurt," Karen would tell Sydney sometimes, when Sydney came over, not to be beaten up, but to cook supper for her, or to just sit on the back porch with her, and to watch the fields.

Sydney would nod whenever Karen said that she still hurt, and he would study his hands.

"I could have grabbed him," he'd say, and then look up and out at the field some more. "I keep thinking that one of these years, I'm going to get a second chance." Sydney would shake his head again. "I think I could have grabbed him," he'd say.

"Or you could have dived in after him," Karen would say, hopefully, wistfully. "Maybe you could have dived in after him."

Her voice would trail off, and her face would be flat and weary.

On these occasions, Sydney Bean wanted the beatings to come once a week, or even daily. But they hurt, too, almost as much as the loss of his friend, and he said nothing. He still felt as if he owed Henry something. He didn't know what.

Sometimes, when he was down on his knees, and Karen was kicking him or elbowing him, he felt close to it—and he almost felt angry at Karen—but he could never catch the shape of it, only the feeling.

He wanted to know what was owed, so he could go on.

On his own farm, there were cattle down in the fields, and they would get lost, separated from one another, and would low all through the night. It was a sound like soft thunder in the night, before the rain comes, and he liked it.

He raised the cattle, and trained horses too: he saddle-broke the young ones that had never been ridden before, the one- and two-year olds, the stallions, the wild mares. That pounding, and the evil, four-footed stamp-and-spin they went into when they could not shake him; when they began to do that, he knew he had them beaten. He charged $250 a horse, and sometimes it took him a month.

Old Dr. Lynly needed a helper, but couldn't pay much, and Sydney, who had done some business with the vet, helped Karen get the job. She needed something to do besides sitting around on her back porch, waiting for the end of each month.

Dr. Lynly was older than Karen had thought he would be, when she met him up close. He had that look to him that told her it might be the last year of his life. It wasn't so much any illness or feebleness or disability. It was just a finished look.

He and Buster—an Airedale, six years old—lived within the city limits of Vicksburg, down below the battlefield, hidden in one of the ravines—his house was up on blocks, the yard flooded with almost every rain—and in his yard, in various corrals and pens, were chickens, ducks, goats, sheep, ponies, horses, cows, and an ostrich. It was illegal to keep them as pets, and the city newspaper editor was after him to get rid of them, but Dr. Lynly claimed they were all being treated by his tiny clinic.

"You're keeping these animals too long, Doc," the editor told him. Dr. Lynly would pretend to be senile, and would pretend to think the editor was asking for a prescription, and would begin quoting various and random chemical names.

The Airedale minded Dr. Lynly exquisitely. He brought the paper, the slippers, he left the room on command, and he brought the chickens' eggs, daily, into the kitchen, making several trips for his and Dr. Lynly's breakfast. Dr. Lynly would have six eggs, fried for himself, and Buster would get a dozen or so, broken into his bowl raw. Any extras went into the refrigerator for Dr. Lynly to take on his rounds, though he no longer had many; only the very oldest people, who remembered him, and the very poorest, who knew he worked for free. They knew he would charge them only for the medicine.

Buster's coat was glossy from the eggs, and burnished, black and tan. His eyes, deep in the curls, were bright, sometimes like the brightest things in the world. He watched Dr. Lynly all the time.

Sometimes Karen watched Dr. Lynly play with Buster, bending down and swatting him in the chest, slapping his shoulders. She had thought it would be mostly kittens and lambs. Mostly, though, he told her, it would be the horses.

The strongest creatures were the ones that got the sickest, and their pain was unspeakable when they finally did yield to it. On the rounds with Dr. Lynly, Karen forgot to think about Henry at all. Though she was horrified by the pain, and almost wished it were hers, bearing it rather than watching it, when the horses suffered.

*O*nce, when Sydney was with her, he had reached out and taken her hand in his. When she looked down and saw it, she had at first been puzzled, not recognizing what it was, and then repulsed, as if it were a giant slug: and she threw Sydney's hand off hers quickly, and ran into her room.

Sydney stayed out on the porch. It was heavy blue twilight and all the cattle down in the fields were feeding.

"I'm sorry," he called out. "But I can't bring him back!" He waited for her to answer, but could only hear her sobs. It had been three years, he thought.

He knew he was wrong to have caught her off-balance like that:

but he was tired of her unhappiness, and frustrated that he could do nothing to end it. The sounds of her crying carried, and the cows down in the fields began to move closer, with interest. The light had dimmed, there were only dark shadows and pale lights, and a low gold thumbnail of a moon—a wet moon—came up over the ragged tear of trees by the bayou.

The beauty of the evening, being on Karen's back porch and in her life, when it should have been Henry, flooded Sydney with a sudden guilt. He had been fighting it, and holding it back, constantly: and then, suddenly, the quietness of the evening, and the stillness, released it.

He heard himself saying a crazy thing.

"I pushed him off, you know," he said, loudly enough so she could hear. "I finished my drink, and put both hands on his skinny-ass little shoulders, and said, 'Take a deep breath, Henry.' I just pushed him off," said Sydney.

It felt good, making up the lie. He was surprised at the relief he felt: it was as if he had control of the situation. It was like when he was on the horses, breaking them, trying to stay on.

Presently, Karen came back out with a small blue pistol, a .38, and she went down the steps and out to where he was standing, and she put it next to his head.

"Let's get in the truck," she said.

He knew where they were going.

The river was about ten miles away, and they drove slowly. There was fog flowing across the low parts of the road and through the fields and meadows like smoke, coming from the woods, and he was thinking about how cold and hard the water would be when he finally hit.

He felt as if he were already falling towards it, the way it had taken Henry forever to fall. But he didn't say anything, and though it didn't feel right, he wondered if perhaps it was this simple, as if this was what was owed after all.

They drove on, past the blue fields and the great spills of fog. The roofs of the hay barns were bright silver polished tin, under the little moon and stars. There were small lakes, cattle stock tanks, and steam rose from them.

They drove with the windows down; it was a hot night, full of flying bugs, and about two miles from the river, Karen told him to stop.

He pulled off to the side of the road, and wondered what she was going to do with his body. A cattle egret flew by, ghostly white and large, flying slowly, and Sydney was amazed that he had never recognized their beauty before, though he had seen millions. It flew right across their windshield, from across the road, and it startled both of them.

The radiator ticked.

"You didn't really push him off, did you?" Karen asked. She still had the pistol against his head, and had switched hands.

Like frost burning off the grass in a bright morning sun, there was in his mind a sudden, sugary, watery feeling—like something dissolving. She was not going to kill him after all.

"No," he said.

"But you could have saved him," she said, for the thousandth time.

"I could have reached out and grabbed him," Sydney agreed. He was going to live. He was going to get to keep feeling things, was going to get to keep seeing things.

He kept his hands in his lap, not wanting to alarm Karen, but his eyes moved all around as he looked for more egrets. He was eager to see another one.

Karen watched him for a while, still holding the pistol against him, and then turned it around and looked at the open barrel of it, cross-eyed, and held it there, right in her face, for several seconds. Then she reached out and put it in the glove box.

Sydney Bean was shuddering.

"Thank you," he said. "Thank you for not shooting yourself."

He put his head down on the steering wheel, in the moonlight, and shuddered again. There were crickets calling all around them. They sat like that for a long time, Sydney leaning against the wheel, and Karen sitting up straight, just looking out at the fields.

Then the cattle began to move up the hill towards them, thinking that Karen's old truck was the one that had come to feed them, and slowly, drifting up the hill from all over the fields, coming from out of the woods, and from their nearby resting spots on the sandbars along the little dry creek that ran down into the bayou—eventually, they all assembled around the truck, like schoolchildren.

They stood there in the moonlight, some with white faces like skulls, all about the same size, and chewed grass and watched the truck. One, bolder than the rest—a yearling black Angus—moved in close, bumped the grill of the truck with his nose, playing, and then leapt back again, scattering some of the others.

"How much would you say that one weighs?" Karen asked. "How much, Sydney?"

They drove the last two miles to the river slowly. It was about four A.M. The yearling cow was bleating and trying to break free; Sydney had tied him up with his belt, and with jumper cables and shoelaces, and an old shirt. His lip was bloody from where the calf had butted him.

But he had wrestled larger steers than that before.

They parked at the old bridge, the one across which the trains still ran. Farther downriver, they could see an occasional car, two round spots of headlight moving slowly and steadily across the new bridge, so far above the river, going very slowly. Sydney put his shoulders under the calf's belly and lifted it with his back and legs, and like a prisoner in the stock, he carried it out to the center of the bridge. Karen followed. It took about fifteen minutes to get there, and Sydney was trembling, dripping with sweat, when finally they gauged they had reached the middle. The deepest part.

They sat there, soothing the frightened calf, stroking its ears, patting its flanks, and waited for the sun to come up. When it did, pale orange behind the great steaminess of the trees and river below—the fog from the river and trees a gunmetal gray, the whole world washed in gray flatness, except for the fruit of the sun—they untied the calf, and pushed him over.

They watched him forever and forever, a black object and then a black spot against the great background of no-colored river, and then there was a tiny white splash, lost almost immediately in the river's current. Logs, which looked like twigs from up on the bridge, swept across the spot. Everything headed south, moving south, and there were no eddies, no pauses.

"I am halfway over him," Karen said.

And then, walking back, she said: "So that was really what it was like?"

She had a good appetite, and they stopped at the Waffle House and ate eggs and pancakes, and had sausage and biscuits and bacon and orange juice. She excused herself to go to the restroom, and when she came back out, her face was washed, her hair brushed and clean-looking. Sydney paid for the meal, and when they stepped outside, the morning was growing hot.

"I have to work today," Karen said, when they got back to her house. "We have to go see about a mule."

"Me, too," said Sydney. "I've got a stallion who thinks he's a bad-ass."

She studied him for a second, and felt like telling him to be careful, but didn't. Something was in her, a thing like hope stirring, and she felt guilty for it.

Sydney whistled, driving home, and tapped his hands on the steering wheel, though the radio did not work.

*D*r. Lynly and Karen drove until the truck wouldn't go any farther, bogged down in the clay, and then they got out and walked. It was cool beneath all the big trees, and the forest seemed to be trying to press in on them. Dr. Lynly carried his heavy bag, stopping and switching arms frequently. Buster trotted slightly ahead, between the two of them, looking left and right, and up the road, and even up into the tops of the trees.

There was a sawmill, deep in the woods, where the delta's farmland in the northern part of the county settled at the river and then went into dark mystery; hardwoods, and muddy roads, then no roads. The men at the sawmill used mules to drag their trees to the cutting. There had never been money for bulldozers, or even tractors. The woods were quiet, and foreboding; it seemed to be a place without sound or light.

When they got near the sawmill, they could hear the sound of axes. Four men, shirtless, in muddy boots with the laces undone, were working on the biggest tree Karen had ever seen. It was a tree too big for chain saws. Had any of the men owned one, the tree would have ruined the saw.

One of the men kept swinging at the tree: putting his back into it, with rhythmic, stroking cuts. The other three stepped back, hitched their pants, and wiped their faces with their forearms.

The fourth man stopped cutting finally. There was no fat on him and he was pale, even standing in the beam of sunlight that was coming down through an opening in the trees—and he looked old; fifty, maybe, or sixty. Some of his fingers were missing.

"The mule'll be back in a minute," he said. He wasn't even breathing hard. "He's gone to bring a load up out of the bottom." He pointed with his ax, down into the swamp.

"We'll just wait," said Dr. Lynly. He bent back and tried to look up at the top of the trees. "Y'all just go right ahead with your cutting."

But the pale muscled man was already swinging again, and the other three, with another tug at their beltless pants, joined in: an odd, pausing drumbeat, as four successive whacks hit the tree; then four more again; and then, almost immediately, the cadence stretching out, growing irregular, as the older man chopped faster.

All around them were the soft pittings, like hail, of tree chips, raining into the bushes. One of the chips hit Buster in the nose, and he rubbed it with his paw, and turned and looked up at Dr. Lynly.

They heard the mule before they saw him: he was groaning, like a person. He was coming up the hill that led out of the swamp; he was coming towards them.

They could see the tops of small trees and saplings shaking as he dragged his load through them. Then they could see the tops of his ears; then his huge head, and after that they saw his chest. Veins raced against the chestnut thickness of it.

Then the tops of his legs.

Then his knee. Karen stared at it and then she started to tremble. She sat down in the mud, and hugged herself—the men stopped swinging, for just a moment—and Dr. Lynly had to help her up.

It was the mule's right knee that was injured, and it had swollen to the size of a basketball. It buckled, with every step he took, pulling the sled up the slick and muddy hill, but he kept his footing and he did not stop. Flies buzzed around the knee, around the infections, where the loggers had pierced the skin with nails and the ends of their knives, trying to drain the pus. Dried blood ran down in streaks to the mule's hoof, to the mud.

The sawlogs on the back of the sled smelled good, fresh. They smelled like they were still alive.

Dr. Lynly walked over to the mule and touched the knee. The mule closed his eyes and trembled slightly, as Karen had done, or even as if in ecstasy, at the chance to rest. The three younger men, plus the sledder, gathered around.

"We can't stop workin' him," the sledder said. "We can't shoot him, either. We've got to keep him alive. He's all we've got. If he dies, it's us that'll have to pull them logs up here."

A cedar moth, from the woods, passed over the mule's ears, fluttering blindly. It rested on the mule's forehead briefly, and then flew off. The mule did not open his eyes. Dr. Lynly frowned and rubbed his chin. Karen felt faint again, and leaned against the mule's sweaty back to keep from falling.

"You sure you've got to keep working him?" Dr. Lynly asked.

"Yes, sir."

The pale logger was still swinging: tiny chips flying in batches.

Dr. Lynly opened his bag. He took out a needle and rag, and a bottle of alcohol. He cleaned the mule's infections. The mule drooled a little when the needle went in, but did not open his eyes. The needle was slender, and it bent and flexed, and slowly Dr. Lynly drained the fluid.

Karen held onto the mule's wet back and vomited into the mud: both her hands on the mule as if she were being arrested against the hood of a car, and her feet spread out wide. The men gripped their axes awkwardly.

Dr. Lynly gave one of them a large plastic jug of pills.

"These will kill his pain," he said. "The knee will get big again, though. I'll be back out, to drain it again." He handed Karen a clean rag from his satchel, and led her away from the mule, away from the mess.

One of the ax men carried their satchel all the way back to the truck. Dr. Lynly let Karen get up into the truck first, and then Buster; then the ax man rocked and shoved, pushing on the hood of the truck as the tires spun, and helped them back it out of the mud: their payment for healing the mule. A smell of burning rubber and smoke hung in the trees after they left.

They didn't talk much. Dr. Lynly was thinking about the pain killers: how for a moment, he had almost given the death pills instead.

Karen was thinking how she would not let him pay her for that day's work. Also she was thinking about Sydney Bean: she would sit on the porch with him again, and maybe drink a beer and watch the fields.

He was sitting on the back porch, when she got in; he was on the wooden bench next to the hammock, and he had a tray set up for her with a pitcher of cold orange juice. There was froth in the pitcher, a light creamy foaminess from where he had been stirring it, and the ice cubes were circling around. Beads of condensation slid down the pitcher, rolling slowly, then quickly, like tears. She could feel her heart giving. The field was rich summer green, and then, past the field, the dark line of trees. A long string of cattle egrets flew past, headed down to their rookery in the swamp.

Sydney poured her a small glass of orange juice. He had a metal pail of cold water and a clean washcloth. It was hot on the back porch, even for evening. He helped her get into the hammock; then he wrung the washcloth out and put it across her forehead, her eyes. Sydney smelled as if he had just gotten out of the shower, and he was wearing clean white duckcloth pants and a bright blue shirt.

She felt dizzy, and leaned back in the hammock. The washcloth over her eyes felt so good. She sipped the orange juice, not looking at it, and licked the light foam of it from her lips. Owls were beginning to call, down in the swamp.

She felt as if she were younger, going back to a place, some place she had not been in a long time but could remember fondly. It felt like she was in love. She knew that she could not be, but that was what it felt like.

Sydney sat behind her and rubbed her temples.

It grew dark, and the moon came up.

"It was a rough day," she said, around ten o'clock.

But he just kept rubbing.

Around eleven o'clock, she dozed off, and he woke her, helped her from the hammock, and led her inside, not turning on any lights, and helped her get in bed.

Then he went back outside, locking the door behind him. He sat on the porch a little longer, watching the moon, so high above him, and then he drove home, slowly, cautiously, as ever. Accidents were everywhere; they could happen at any time, from any direction.

Sydney moved carefully, and tried to look ahead and be ready for the next one.

He really wanted her. He wanted her in his life. Sydney didn't know if the guilt was there for that—the wanting—or because he was alive, still seeing things, still feeling. He wanted someone in his life, and it didn't seem right to feel guilty about it. But he did.

Sometimes, at night, he would hear the horses running, thundering across the hard summer-baked flatness of his pasture, running wild—and he would imagine they were laughing at him for wasting his time feeling guilty, but it was a feeling he could not shake, could not ride down, and his sleep was often poor and restless.

Sydney often wondered if horses were even meant to be ridden at all.

It was always such a struggle.

The thing about the broncs, he realized—and he never realized it until they were rolling on top of him in the dust, or rubbing him off against a tree, or against the side of a barn, trying to break his leg—was that if the horses didn't get broken, tamed, they'd get wilder. There was nothing as wild as a horse that had never been broken. It just got meaner, each day.

So he held on. He bucked and spun and arched and twisted, shooting up and down with the mad horses' leaps; and when the horse tried to hurt itself, by running straight into something—a fence, a barn, the lake—he stayed on.

If there was, once in a blue moon, a horse not only stronger, but more stubborn than he, then he would have to destroy it.

The cattle were easy to work with, they would do anything for food, and once one did it, they would all follow; but working with the horses made him think ahead, and sometimes he wondered, in streaks and bits of paranoia, if perhaps all the horses in the world did not have some battle against him, and were destined, all of them, to pass through his corrals, each one testing him before he was allowed to stop.

Because like all bronc-busters, that was what Sydney someday allowed himself to consider and savor, in moments of rest: the day when he could stop. A run of successes. A string of wins so satisfying and continuous that it would seem—even though he would be sore, and tired—that a horse would never beat him again, and he would be convinced of it, and then he could quit.

Mornings in summers past, Henry used to come over, and sit on the railing and watch. He had been an elementary school teacher, and frail, almost anemic: but he had lovedz to watch Sydney Bean ride the horses. He taught only a few classes in the summers, and he would sip coffee and grade a few papers while Sydney and the horse fought out in the center.

Sometimes Henry had set a broken bone for Sydney—Sydney had shown him how—and other times Sydney, if he was alone, would set his own bones, if he even bothered with them. Then he would wrap them up and keep riding. Dr. Lynly had set some of his bones, on the bad breaks.

Sydney was feeling old, since Henry had drowned. Not so

much in the mornings, when everything was new and cool, and
had promise; but in the evenings, he could feel the crooked shapes
of his bones, within him. He would drink beers, and watch his
horses, and other people's horses in his pasture, as they ran. The
horses never seemed to feel old, not even in the evenings, and he
was jealous of them, of their strength.

*H*e called Karen one weekend. "Come out and watch me
break horses," he said.

He was feeling particularly sore and tired. For some reason he
wanted her to see that he could always do it; that the horses were
always broken. He wanted her to see what it looked like, and how
it always turned out.

"Oh, I don't know," she said, after she had considered it. "I'm
just so *tired.*" It was a bad and crooked road, bumpy, from her
house to his, and it took nearly an hour to drive it.

"I'll come get you . . . ?" he said. He wanted to shake her. But
he said nothing; he nodded, and then remembered he was on the
phone and said, "I understand."

*S*he did let him sit on the porch with her, whenever he drove
over to her farm. She had to have someone.

"Do you want to hit me?" he asked one evening, almost hopefully.

But she just shook her head sadly.

He saw that she was getting comfortable with her sorrow, was
settling down into it, like an old way of life, and he wanted to
shock her out of it, but felt paralyzed and mute, like the dumbest
of animals.

Sydney stared at his crooked hands, with the scars from the
cuts, made over the years by the fencing tools. Silently, he cursed
all the many things he did not know. He could lift bales of hay.

He could string barbed-wire fences. He could lift things. That was all he knew. He wished he were a chemist, an electrician, a poet, or a preacher. The things he had—what little of them there were—wouldn't help her.

She had never thought to ask how drunk Henry had been. Sydney thought that made a difference: whether you jumped off the bridge with one beer in you, or two, or a six-pack; or with a sea of purple Psychos rolling around in your stomach—but she never asked.

He admired her confidence, and doubted his ability to be as strong, as stubborn. She never considered that it might have been her fault, or Henry's; that some little spat might have prompted it, or general disillusionment.

It was his fault, Sydney's, square and simple, and she seemed comfortable, if not happy, with the fact.

Dr. Lynly treated horses, but he did not seem to love them, thought Karen.

"Stupid creatures," he would grumble, when they would not do as he wanted, when he was trying to doctor them. "Utter idiots." He and Buster and Karen would try to herd the horse into the trailer, or the corral, pulling on the reins and swatting the horse with green branches.

"Brickheads," Dr. Lynly would growl, pulling the reins and then walking around and slapping, feebly, the horse's flank. "Brickheads and fatheads." He had been loading horses for fifty years, and Karen would giggle, because the horses' stupidity always seemed to surprise, and then anger Dr. Lynly, and she thought it was sweet.

It was as if he had not yet really learned that that was how they always were.

But Karen had seen that right away. She knew that a lot of girls, and women, were infatuated with horses, in love with them even, for their great size and strength, and for their wildness—but Karen, as she saw more and more of the sick horses, the ailing ones, the ones most people did not see regularly, knew that all horses were dumb, simple and trusting, and that even the smartest ones could be made to do as they were told.

And they could be so dumb, so loyal, and so oblivious to pain. It was if—even if they could feel it—they could never, ever acknowledge it.

It was sweet, she thought, and dumb.

*K*aren let Sydney rub her temples and brush her hair. She would go into the bathroom, and wash it while he sat on the porch. He had taken up whittling; one of the stallions had broken Sydney's leg by throwing him into a fence and then trampling him, and the leg was in a heavy cast. So Sydney had decided to take a break for a few days.

He had bought a whittling kit at the hardware store, and was going to try hard to learn how to do it. There were instructions. The kit had a square, light piece of balsa wood, almost the weight of nothing, and a plain curved whittling knife. There was a dotted outline in the shape of a duck's head on the balsa wood that showed what the shape of his finished work would be.

After he learned to whittle, Sydney wanted to learn to play the harmonica. That was next, after whittling.

He would hear the water running, and hear Karen splashing, as she put her head under the faucet and rinsed.

She would come out in her robe, drying her hair, and then would let him sit in the hammock with her and brush her hair. It was September, and the cottonwoods were tinging, were making the skies hazy, soft and frozen. Nothing seemed to move.

Her hair came down to the middle of her back. She had stopped cutting it. The robe was old and worn, the color of an old blue dish. Something about the shampoo she used reminded him of apples. She wore moccasins that had a shearling lining in them, and Sydney and Karen would rock in the hammock, slightly. Sometimes Karen would get up and bring out two Cokes from the refrigerator, and they would drink those.

"Be sure to clean up those shavings when you go," she told him. There were little balsa wood curls all over the porch. Her hair, almost dry, would be light and soft. "Be sure not to leave a mess when you go," she would say.

It would be dark then, Venus out beyond them.

"Yes," he said.

Before he left, she reached out from the hammock, and caught his hand. She squeezed it, and then let go.

He drove home slowly, thinking of Henry, and of how he had once taken Henry fishing for the first time. They had caught a catfish so large that it had scared Henry. They drank beers, and sat in the boat, and talked.

One of Sydney Bean's headlights faltered, on the drive home, then went out, and it took him an hour and a half to get home.

*T*he days got cold and brittle. It was hard, working with the horses: Sydney's leg hurt all the time. Sometimes the horse would leap, and come down with all four hooves bunched in close together, and the pain and shock of it would travel all the way up Sydney's leg and into his shoulder, and down into his wrists: the break was in his ankle.

He was sleeping past sun-up, some days, and was being thrown, now, nearly every day; sometimes several times in the same day.

There was always a strong wind. Rains began to blow in. It was cool, getting cold, crisp as apples, and it was the weather that in the summer everyone said they would be looking forward to. One night there was a frost, and a full moon.

On her back porch, sitting in the hammock by herself with a heavy blanket around her, Karen saw a stray balsa shaving caught between the cracks of her porch floor. It was white, in the moonlight—the whole porch was—and the field was blue—the cattle stood out in the moonlight like blue statues—and she almost called Sydney.

She even went as far as to get up and call information, to find out his number; it was that close.

But then the silence and absence of a thing—she presumed it was Henry, but did not know for sure what it was—closed in around her, and the field beyond her porch, like the inside of her heart, seemed to be deathly still—and she did not call.

She thought angrily, I can love who I want to love. But she was angry at Sydney Bean, for having tried to pull her so far out, into a place where she did not want to go.

She fell asleep in the hammock, and dreamed that Dr. Lynly was trying to wake her up, and was taking her blood pressure, feeling her forehead, and, craziest of all, swatting at her with green branches.

She awoke from the dream, and decided to call him after all. Sydney answered the phone as if he, too, had been awake.

"Hello?" he said. She could tell by the true questioning in his voice that he did not get many phone calls.

"Hello," said Karen. "I just—wanted to call, and tell you hello." She paused; almost a falter. "And that I feel better. That I feel good, I mean. That's all."

"Well," said Sydney Bean. "well, good. I mean, great."

"That's all," said Karen. "Bye," she said.

"Good-bye," said Sydney.

On Thanksgiving Day, Karen and Dr. Lynly headed back out to the swamp, to check up on the loggers' mule. It was the hardest cold of the year, and there was bright ice on the bridges, and it was not thawing, even in the sun. The inside of Dr. Lynly's old truck was no warmer than the air outside. Buster, in his wooliness, lay across Karen to keep her warm.

They turned onto a gravel road, and started down into the swamp. Smoke, low and spreading, was all in the woods, like a fog. The men had little fires going all throughout the woods; they were each working on a different tree, and had small warming fires where they stood and shivered when resting.

Karen found herself looking for the pale ugly logger.

He was swinging the ax, but he only had one arm, he was swinging at the tree with one arm. The left arm was gone, and there was a sort of a sleeve over it, like a sock. The man was sweating, and a small boy stepped up and quickly toweled him dry each time the pale man stepped back to take a rest.

They stopped the truck and got out and walked up to him, and he stepped back—wet, already, again; the boy toweled him off, standing on a low stool and starting with the man's neck and shoulders, and then going down the great back—and the man told them that the mule was better but that if they wanted to see him, he was lower in the swamp.

They followed the little path towards the river. All around them were downed trees, and stumps, and stacks of logs, but the woods looked no different. The haze from the fires made it seem colder. Acorns popped under their feet.

About halfway down the road, they met the mule. He was coming back up towards them, and he was pulling a good load. A small boy was in front of him, holding out a carrot, only partially eaten. The mule's knee looked much better, though it was still a little swollen, and probably always would be.

The boy stopped, and let the mule take another bite of carrot, making him lean far forward in the trace. His great rubbery lips stretched and quavered, and then flapped, as he tried to get it, and then there was the crunch when he did.

They could smell the carrot as the mule ground it with his old teeth. It was a wild carrot, dug from the woods, and not very big: but it smelled good.

Karen had brought an apple and some sugar cubes, and she started forward to give them to the mule, but instead, handed them to the little boy, who ate the sugar cubes himself, and put the apple in his pocket.

The mule was wearing an old straw hat, and looked casual, out-of-place. The boy switched him, and he shut his eyes and started up: his chest swelled, tight and sweaty, to fit the dark soft stained leather harness, and the big load behind him started in motion, too.

Buster whined, as the mule went by.

*I*t was spring again then, the month in which Henry had left them, and they were on the back porch. Karen had purchased a Clydesdale yearling, a great and huge animal, whose mane and fur she had shaved to keep it cool in the warming weather, and she had asked a little boy from a nearby farm with time on his hands to train it, in the afternoons. The horse was already gentled, but needed to be stronger. She was having the boy walk him around in the fields, pulling a makeshift sled of stones and tree stumps and old rotten bales of hay.

In the fall, when the Clydesdale was strong enough, she and Dr. Lynly were going to trailer it out to the swamp, and trade it for the mule.

Sydney Bean's leg had healed, been broken again, and was now healing once more. The stallion he was trying to break was showing signs of weakening. There was something in the whites of his eyes, Sydney thought, when he reared up, and he was not slamming himself into the barn—so it seemed to Sydney, anyway— with quite as much anger. Sydney thought that perhaps this coming summer would be the one in which he broke all of his horses, day after day, week after week.

They sat in the hammock and drank Cokes and nibbled radishes, celery, which Karen had washed and put on a little tray. They watched the boy, or one of his friends, his blue shirt a tiny spot against the treeline, as he followed the big dark form of the Clydesdale. The sky was a wide spread of crimson, all along the western trees, towards the river. They couldn't tell which of the local children it was, behind the big horse; it could have been any of them.

"I really miss him," said Sydney Bean. "I really hurt."

"I know," Karen said. She put her hand on Sydney's, and rested it there. "I will help you," she said.

Out in the field, a few cattle egrets fluttered and hopped behind the horse and and boy. The great young draft horse lifted his thick legs high and free of the mud with each step, free from the mud made soft by the rains of spring, and slowly—they could tell—he was skidding the sled forward.

The egrets hopped and danced, following at a slight distance, but neither the boy nor the horse seemed to notice. They kept their heads down, and moved forward.

THE GOVERNMENT BEARS

$\smile$

My name is D. W. Pitts, and I am nearing sixty years old. I was fifty-nine in last October. I shot a deer for my people the day we were to have a full moon that month. I cleaned him right before dusk, and then the wind changed that night and opened all the clouds up to crystal stars and we had the first frost, not melting but freezing even harder and like snow in the morning: a bright sun, and the shock of another year, even to the young ones. There are three of them, and my son, Ray, and his woman, Becca. I try as hard as I can to keep everyone fed and to make sure the young ones notice dandelions, dockweed, owls, and horses. There is no greater joy than children.

The little girl, Alice, is four and blonde, already with glasses. I sold the Jeep to buy her the glasses. The twins are six, and mean, and stubblesouled. Nothing will ever hurt them. They will demolish this state. With the twins around me, there is no harshness in the world. Not anymore. Ray's a drunkard. I chuckle when I think of the twins, and unleashing them. I hate this state sometimes. I must not let them be changed.

When I was twenty-seven I was hit in the head by a man wielding a fourteen-inch pipe wrench. He was about a hundred pounds heavier than I was. Sometimes when I throw two fifty-pound sacks of feed out of the truck and listen to them hit I think about that. He was much larger than I was but I killed him.

It wasn't even over some woman, or a horse or a dog, or our mothers' names: it was just plain bad blood, that odd thing, right from the very start. I had worked with him about a week, and one day he said he didn't like me because my clothes were always too clean and because he said he had seen me looking down the creek like a crazy man, just watching it, when there was nothing there, in the middle of the summer. We were working up on the Big Black, drilling Tinsley Field: cotton everywhere, and the magic in flat sky. Honeysuckle crept and smelled good right on down and into the creek: the water was muddy, and alligators lived in there. If you watched, you could see one every now and then.

I was on my lunch break, and when I finished my sandwich and came back up on the rig floor, he said that stuff to me and then picked up the wrench and came down on top of my head as if trying to cleave me in two. We were circulating out a little peeing mud and he and I were the only ones up there on the floor and there was all this blood in my eyes all of a sudden. It was in my face and mouth too. It was sticky and I thought it was my brain—I could smell this odor like fried or burned okra: I thought that was my mind, exposed to the sunlight. I grabbed the coffee-pot and shorted it out and skittered it across the derrick floor, across the mud, and into the trip gas. It blew the rig to kingdom come and I woke up in the brush down by the creek with a broken cheek and collarbone and twisted ankles and some rig metal in my chest and thigh. No one knew much about the field back in those days. They said it would just pee a little; they said it wouldn't blow.

Now I live down near Laurel. There may not be enough good I can do the rest of my life to make up for killing that man.

I still limp. My state will always limp. I keep the kids here, truthfully, because I have no say in it; Ray will not move. The people here will eat them up, or try. But above all I would rather that than the children merge with them, and take on their rampant nastiness, hatred of self, love of disaster. Above all I must keep the children above this.

*W*hen Ray was little the children called him the Killer's Son. This was before we moved to Laurel. Then God took his mother: we were driving, all of us, west of Vicksburg in this old Ford and the axle broke and we went into some trees. In school, after we were both out of the hospital, the children told him I had killed his mother too. Shortly after he was married, his first woman caught this disease from another man and hanged herself in this other man's kitchen.

My family's snake-bit. Since I got struck by the pipe wrench and blew up the rig in anger, this state's never given me any trouble directly but it's sure taken it out on my kin.

I must prepare the boys well.

Very few nations have had a war fought in their very own backyard, and certainly no other American states, not like us, not like Mississippi. I don't care if it was a hundred and twenty years ago, these things still last and that is really no time at all, not for a real war like that one, with screaming and pain. The trees absorb the echoes of the screams and cries and humiliations. Their bark is only an inch thick between the time then and now: the distance between your thumb and forefinger. The sun beating down on us now saw the flames and troops' campfires then, and in fact the warmth from those flames is still not entirely through traveling to the sun. The fear of the women: you can still feel it, in places where it was strong.

I give it at least another hundred to wash out entirely. You can get on a raft on the Big Black River and float down the chocolate milk color of it in the middle of summer with the cicadas' mad screaming, and there is no difference between then and now. Not yet. We were men, humans, countrymen, fighting among our own unlike selves. I can feel a crease in my head, down the center, like the mail slot in a door. Sometimes I will hear a sizzling sound, like a power line, or live wire: it comes from inside my head. I can hear it (sometimes) when all else is silent. Some foods have no taste. Others taste like rotting, garlicky flesh: and yet I steal looks around, and everyone else is eating normally. I do need to stay alive to see the twins make it through all right.

I move fairly carefully, and do not jump from wagons, or from the back of the truck. This is the state that invented hacking somebody up and putting them in little bags in the freezer: this sort of mess is always going on down around Columbia and the coast, in the weekend papers. They pure and simply hate everything down here. Not any great remorse or shame at having been wrong, but the plain ugly embarrassment of having been beaten at something. A biological reaction. The knowledge is in our genes.

There are bears in our woods, down around the blue ridges and forests of Laurel, not Faulkner's bears, but postdepression government bears, little thirty- and forty-pound dwarf things the government put in there, genetically trapped in their sorrowful size forever, to deal with the pigs. Because there is a lot of government pulpwood and timber down there and the scores of wild pigs were running through the woods tusking and ripping basically at everything in sight, cutting trails through the woods in their natural and musky continuous anger. These little government bears were going to do the trick. They were bred to not get large enough to attack the pigs, most of which were three or four times their size. The bears' strong point, said the government, was their quickness, and that they would follow the mother pigs forever and then eat all the little young pigs out of the nest.

Eventually the pigs ate up all the timber they wanted and then there was a war and we cut and logged most of the rest (Ray lost a thumb), and then we plowed a good bit of the leftover into marshy farmland, these ovals and patches of corn in the wilderness, tractor rows furrowing right alongside and next to some still-standing groves and dark forest—near the heavy creeks, and down in the hollows—so that you can be a sodbuster and still hear alligators too, while farming, or be unhitching the mules, and step from bright farmer's heat into the dark woods. I'm not sure I don't like it better that way than how it was all woods, before. The little government bears still live in the woods and are forever clowning around: eating corn, racing in packs of five and six down the trails like schoolchildren, black as the earthen footpaths, excited, mischievous, racing down the trails.

*B*ecca loves to garden. She puts up with Ray. She honors him, and remembers who he was. He paws her, grabs at her behind through her dress, sometimes: she bustles past. Out to pick okra; off to feed the horses. She has strawberry hair and loves the horses. I have seen her hugging them. I think everyone has to do one really bad thing in life to call their life a life, and if I had not killed the man I would probably entertain taking my son's wife from him and the children too and starting over. Or would have, ten years ago, anyway. Back when he started drinking. The children may not be his; I don't know. I remember when Becca was big with the twins, big and feeding the horses, I was thinking this for no real reason and looked at her while I was thinking it and she saw it and looked quickly away, but I don't know, I'm not much good with women, she may merely have been batting at a horsefly. My own wife and I had a special sort of trust and strength but then I didn't want to buy a new truck, thought we could get by on the old one, and that was the end of that relationship. We sure do eat a lot of potatoes.

Something always comes up though. I should probably stop worrying about it and have a little faith. I am good with engines (I know how to short coffee-pots). I bought the twins two red three-wheelers with burned-out valves and re-ground them, and now they run wild and strong again. I'm a provider. I refuse to believe in this business about my family being cursed for my wrong. This manure about the sins of the fathers and how they in any way can affect (adversely) the lives of their sons and daughters is just not so. You do for yourself: you make your own breaks, and pull yourself up, or stay down, depending entirely and only on what you want.

I can provide anything. Maybe some day even I will be able to afford one of those satellite dishes in the front yard for Ray, so he can lie there in his bed and never leave, just rot away, with a hundred and seventeen different lives to choose from other than the own miserable one he is choosing for himself. Yeah, he'd like that. And oh, the kids would turn out real good then, yeah, sure.

But I shouldn't talk. It's wrong to judge, even my own son. Those three-wheelers will probably be the death of the little twins before anything. They ride them like electrons, clinging to them; they curse, they give it full throttle. They're so little, and get so caught up in it (no fear) that they sometimes forget to shift up, to change gears. They'll wind those little re-bored engines up tighter than a buzz saw, just zing-whining up and over the fields (bumping across furrows, logs, leaving the ground from a natural ramp in a leap over the irrigation creek: I'm flying! I'm flying! Look, Ma, I'm flying!—looking back over their shoulders grinning, teeth missing, not even looking to where they're going to land) (Everything will be all right) and I'll have to shout at the lead one from my work, hoeing or weeding, or planting, "Change gears, dummy!" and if it's Arthur, he'll look down and remember and stick his tongue out the side of his mouth and pop it up a notch, and then immediately look back and shout, sternly, at Andrew: "Hey, change gears, dummy!"

To Becca's credit, she lets them go: she sees their happiness, their utter levitation, and rests her head on the horse's shoulder, or leans on the hoe, and watches them, wistfully: not wistful that she could be doing it, too, but wistful that it is necessary to want them to be free, and in a better world, and a more complete happiness, as long as it can last. That she has to let them risk their lives and injuries, in order to have the lives and health she wants for them. They wear little blue crash helmets, blurs of colors when they are screaming through the woods, and elbow pads and tiny boots, and get up swearing when they crash. My head hurts when I hear them swear like their classmates have taught them: I do not want them to grow up to be the same—angry and obscene, like the rest of this defeated, backwoods state—but different.

Things that are different must be strong. Things that are different will be told, and tried to be made, to yield. The little government bears are very hard to encounter, when you have a gun, but every year the hunters around here will bag a few, come driving or walking in with their pitiful smallness, maybe two or three of them slung over their shoulders, the hunters' eyes glazed and tongues thick with a fungoid of self-congratulations and jackoff: having killed a Bear, you know.

Myself, I've seen the bears pretty often. They're on to me; they know the difference between camouflage green and army boots and me just leaning on my hoe, suspenders, a straw hat, no shirt, a day's smell upon my body. When the evening gets cool I see them often. They don't bother my fields, largely because I'm always working, but also because of the fury of the twins and the three-wheelers, but I've been out walking—on Sundays, when I take the day off—and seen them raiding others' fields. I've seen as many as fourteen of them in a field at a time, teeth clicking and corn stalks waving and falling like some unleashed nether-world force is in them. The little government bears will run in shifts, back to the woods, on three legs, carrying as much corn as they can hold under their fourth arm, tucked up against their body. Except if they drop a piece, say, crossing the fence and back into the woods, they'll look at it and then, as if saying ah, shit, they'll let go of all of it, all the corn, and hurry back to the cornfield and pick up another load. Corn strewn *everywhere,* by night's approach.

There is no compromising, in those little government bears. Hunters will never be able to get all of them out of the woods.

"*M*ama, mama, Goose has done took over the yard!" Their eyes are big. Comic. Earnest. Disbelieving. Asking their mother, What next? A mean goose, unruly in the yard for no sudden reason, routing the dog, the horse, even the twins. Goose has done took over. I'm eating breakfast, gumming grits, about to go out and plow, ever plow. Alice is sitting with me, and watches the boys with something beyond worship: the Twins! Where is hers? It is good that they go to their mother for permission, for issuance of news. Arthur has a hideous purple twist mark on his forearm, and Andrew, as if feeling his brother's pain, is muttering damn, damn, damn, very seriously, and smacking his fist against the palm of his hand. Look out, goose.

"Protect yourself!" she says. It is a cliché; she is wiping her hands on her apron. The sun through the kitchen window is making her hair look angelic. "Whup his button, and good," she tells them. They look at each other. Mother has spoken. If nothing else they have learned obedience to her.

Out in the field. Already sweating. The goose comes racing by, head stretched full out and flat to the ground, honking, bleating, a thing fearful for the first time, and in thirty-three years I have learned nothing, I am laughing, they are right on his tail running him down into the swamp with feathers flying and it is the goose's eyes that are bugging now, great loud red Bigger Gooses after him now, two of them, and everything will turn on you, everything, if you live long enough—even good and bad luck. We must hope. The goose lay down there in the swamp all afternoon, exhausted, a muddy has-been, and before dusk I had to go get him and carry him up to the house, where I ousted the dog and put him in the kennel and locked the gate, to protect him from his enemies: the baleful hound, the pride-injured horses.

The twins were gleeful, victorious, proud, and just-turned six. The goose was a candy goose, a broken thing, and later that year we ate him at Thanksgiving with righteousness. Andrew said the prayer and told God he guessed we showed that goose's ass. Ray didn't make it out of bed. It rained. Then turned cold. The wind blew a hole in the roof. Andrew said he wanted to learn how to chew tobacco. I looked at Becca and my eyes said, I hate this state. And her eyes looked at me and said, Ray will never leave. I passed her the goose.

My own son is taking a lifetime draught of self-pity and rolling around in his sorrow like a blind paralyzed baby opossum. Some days smell like death and tears. There's a lady three miles down the road who handles snakes in her church services and I swear that takes less courage than to just duck your head and keep on doing what you are doing, the regular.

*A*nother neighbor killed an elk once. In Mississippi. Coming up the creek. He'd been seeing its tracks, and didn't know what it was. Asked the game warden about it. The warden told him it was an elk, sure enough, and had escaped from this rich man's farm. They'd been trying to trap it as it moved north, Thompson Creek, Pool Creek, Wausau Creek . . . if they didn't get it before summer and treat it, hot parasites would kill it. My neighbor was on a tree stand when he saw the elk; it was kind of staggering up the creek, already skeletal looking, and he shot him. Got his picture in the paper. He had elk steaks. I hate this state.

They won't tolerate anything different. That, more than anything, drives me to encourage the boys. Fit in where you don't: make your own space. I *want* them to be different. So that they don't give in.

Exist somewhere you're not supposed to, or where you don't want to. Be your own men; do what you want, and don't hurt anybody. What a real and utter victory that would be, the only and best victory.

The boys have never seen the government bears. I can only hope that they will stare and wonder, maybe even marvel, but not shoot. Maybe even catch a glimpse of themselves. And of the bears' greatness and earned freedom.

*M*y head hurts. But I've got to work. I've got to keep the twins and Alice fed. Becca can't do it all herself. So they don't show much resemblance to Ray. Who can blame her for wanting to escape, if only for a moment, like the twins over the irrigation ditch? Who can blame her?

Little Alice has a cough; little Alice is always coughing. Always, the story remains the same. We will make it through somehow. She sleeps with a cotton gauze tent draped all around her bed; she comes to the porch in the butter sunlight, squinting or perhaps wincing, and watches the boys. Her feet are bare; her hand is dirty, and in her mouth. I leave the field and go to her and pick her up and kiss her; my straw hat shades her, and makes her laugh.

Makes her laugh. You should always make children laugh. She has a pet chicken called Flute. We will not eat Flute.

*T*he wind, when a storm is coming, ruffles the hair on the back of my neck: even in the summer, chills the sweat, assuages my head, makes me shiver. The crops are pale water-colored green; the trees at their edges, dark forest color. Ray's radio plays from back at the house faintly, its voice and message indescribable and meaningless as the birds begin to fly low in response to the plunge in barometer. It begins to rain. The crops will do well. There is nothing as good as standing in the middle of crops in the summer as it rains. I lean on my hoe and it slicks my hair down and soothes me.

The children are amused. But even already, the boys show some slight mistrustful hint of understanding, of what is to come: they do not laugh nearly as hard as Alice.

*T*he other night I had a dream. I will live forever. I was seventy-five years old and was in a meadow, listening to my children's children's laughter. Children I had never seen before were laughing, playing, running. Everything was different, in the dream, than it is now. There were these white pastel flowers all in the field. Times were so good that we had decided not to even plant, that year. I was holding a glass of wine. Becca was smiling. Ray was sober.

Off in the dark woods, trouble hid. It was so far away that it seemed it would never return.

REDFISH

Cuba Libres are made with rum, diet Coke, and lime juice. Kirby showed them to me, and someone, I am sure, showed them to him. They've probably been around forever, the way everything has. But the first time we really drank them was late at night on the beach in Galveston. There was a high wind coming off the water, and we had a fire roaring. I think that it felt good for Kirby to be away from Tricia for a while and I know that it felt good to be away from Houston.

We were fishing for red drum—redfish—and somewhere, out in the darkness, beyond where we could see, we had hurled our hooks and sinkers, baited with live shrimp. There was a big moon and the waves blew spray into our faces and we wore heavy coats, and our faces were orange, to one another, from the light of the big driftwood fire.

It is amazing, what washes in from the ocean. Everything in the world ends up, I think, on a beach. Whales, palm trees, television sets. . . . Kirby and I were sitting on a couch in the sand drinking the Cuba Libres and watching our lines, waiting for the big redfish to hit. When he did, or she, we were going to reel it in and then clean it there on the beach, rinse it off in the waves, and then we were going to grill it, on the big driftwood fire.

It was our first time to drink Cuba Libres, and we liked them even better than margaritas. We had never caught redfish before, either, but had read about it in a book. We had bought the couch for ten dollars at a garage sale earlier in the day. We sank down deep into it and it was easy, comfortable fishing. In the morning, when the tide started to go out, we were going to wade-fish for speckled trout. We had read about that, too, and that was the way you were supposed to do it. You were supposed to go out into the waves after them. It sounded exciting. We had bought waders and saltwater fishing licenses and saltwater stamps, as well as the couch and the rum. We were going to get into a run of speckled trout and catch our limit, and load the ice chest with them, and take them back to Tricia, because Kirby had made her mad.

But first we were going to catch a big redfish. We wouldn't tell her about the redfish, we decided. We would grill it and drink more Cuba Libres and maybe take a short nap, before the tide changed, and we had our sleeping bags laid out on the sand for that purpose. They looked as if they had been washed ashore, too. It was December, and about thirty degrees. We were on the southeast end of the bay and the wind was strong. The flames from the fire were ten or twelve feet high, but we couldn't get warm.

There was all the wood in the world, huge beams from ships and who-knows-what, and we could make the fire as large as we wanted. We kept waiting for the big redfish to sieze our shrimp and run, to scoot back down into the depths. The book said they were bottom feeders.

It seemed, drinking the Cuba Libres, that it would happen at any second. Kirby and Trish had gotten in a fight because Kirby had forgotten to feed the dogs that Saturday, while Trish was at work. Kirby said, drinking the Cuba Libres, that he had told her that what she was really mad about was the fact that she had to work that Saturday, while he had had the day off. (They both work in a bank, different banks, and handle money, and own sports cars.) Tricia had gotten really mad at that and had refused to feed the dogs.

So Kirby fed his dog but did not feed Tricia's. That was when Tricia got the maddest. Then they got into a fight about how Kirby's dog, a German Shepherd, ate so much more, about ten times more, than did Tricky Woodles, a Cocker spaniel, Tricia's dog. Good old Tricky Woo.

On the beach, Kirby had a pocketbook that identified fishes of the Gulf Coast, and after each drink we would look at it, turning to the page with the picture of the red drum. We would study it, sitting there on the couch, as if we were in high school again, and were studying for some silly exam, instead of being out in the real world, braving the elements, tackling nature, fishing for the mighty red drum. The book said they could go as much as thirty pounds.

"The elusive red drum!" Kirby shouted into the wind. We were only sipping the Cuba Libres, because they were so good, but they were adding up. They were new, and we had just discovered them, and we wanted as many of them as we could get.

"Elusive *and* wily!" I shouted. "Red E. Fish!"

Kirby's eyes darted and shifted like a cartoon character's, the way they did when he was really drunk, which meant he would be passing out soon.

"We could dynamite the ocean," he said. "We could throw grenades into the waves, and stun the fish. They would come rolling in with the waves then, all the fish in the world."

He stood up, fell in the sand, and still on his knees, poured another drink. "I really want to see one," he said.

We left our poles and wandered down the beach: jumping and stamping, it was so cold. The wind tried to blow us over. We found an ancient, upright lifeguard's tower, about twenty feet tall, and tried, in our drunkenness, to pull it down, to drag over to our fire. It was as sturdy as iron, and had barnacles on it, from where it had spent some time in the sea. We cut our hands badly, but it was dark and cold, and we did not find that out until later.

We were a long way from our fire, and it looked a lot smaller, from where we were. The couch looked wrong, without us in it, sitting there by the fire, empty like that. Kirby started crying and said he was going home to Tricia but I told him to buck up and be a man. I didn't know what that meant or even what I meant by saying that, but I knew that I did not want him to leave. We had come in his car, the kind everyone our age in Houston drove, if they had a job, if they had even a little money—a white BMW—and I wanted to stay, and see what a red drum looked like in the flesh.

"I've an idea," I said. "Let's pull the tower down, and drag it over to the fire with the car."

"Yeah!" said Kirby. "Yeah!" Clouds were hurrying past the moon, something was blowing in quickly, but I could see that Kirby had straightened up some, and that he was not going to pass out.

It's been ten years since we were in high school. Some days, when I am with him, it seems that eternity still lies out in front of us; and other days, it seems that we've already died, somehow, and everything is over. Tricia is beautiful. She reminds me of that white sports car.

We kicked most of the sand off of our shoes, and got in the car, and it started right up, the way it always did. It was a nice car, all right, and Kirby drove it to work every day—though work was only one-point-eight miles away—and he kept his briefcase in the back seat; but in the trunk, just thrown in, were all of the things he had always kept in his trunk in high school, things he thought he might need in an emergency.

There was a bow and arrows, a .22 rifle, a tomahawk, binoculars, a tire inflator, a billy club, some extra fishing poles, a tool box, some barbed wire, a bull riding rope, cowboy boots, a wrinkled, oily tuxedo which he had rented and never bothered to return, and there were other things, too—but it was the bull riding rope, which we attached to the tower, and to the back bumper of the little sports car, that came in handy this time.

Sand flew as the tires spun, and like some shy animal, the BMW quickly buried itself, up to the doors.

To the very end, I think Kirby believed that at any moment he was going to pull free, and break out of the sand, and pull the tower over: the engine screaming, the car shuddering and bucking . . . but it was sunk deep, when he gave up, and he had to crawl out through the window.

The Cuba Libres, and the roar of the wind, made it seem funny; we howled, as if it was something the car had done by itself, on its own.

"Let's take a picture and send it to Tricia," he said. I laughed, and winced too, a little, because I thought it was a bad sign that he was talking about her again, so much, so often, but he was happy, so we got the camera from the trunk, and because he did not have a flash attachment, we built another fire, stacked wood there by the tower, which is what we should have done in the first place.

We went back to get the couch, and our poles and sleeping bags, and the ice chest. I had worked, for a while, for a moving company, and I knew a trick so that I could carry on my back a couch, a refrigerator, or almost anything, and I showed it to Kirby, and he screamed, laughing, as I ran down the beach with the couch on my back, not able to see where I was going, carrying the couch like an ant with a leaf, coming dangerously close to the water. Kirby ran along behind me, screaming, carrying the other things, and when we had set up a new camp, we ran back and forth, carrying the larger pieces of burning logs, transferring the fire, too. We took a picture of the car by firelight.

Our hands and arms had dried blood on them almost all the way up to the elbows, from the barnacles, and we rinsed them off in the sea, which was not as cold as we had expected.

"I wish Tricia was here to see this," he said, more than once. The wind was blowing still harder, and the moon was gone entirely.

We got a new fire started, and were exhausted from all the effort; we fixed more drinks and slumped into the couch and raised our poles to cast out again, but stopped, realizing that the shrimp were gone; that something had stolen them.

The other shrimp were in a live well, in the trunk, so we re-baited. It was fun, reaching in the dark into the warm bubbling water of the bait bucket, and feeling the wild tiny shrimp leap about, fishtailing, trying to escape. It didn't matter which shrimp you got; you didn't even need to look. You just reached in, and caught whichever one leapt into your hand.

We baited the hooks, and cast out again. We were thirsty, so we fixed more drinks. We nodded off on the couch, and were awakened by the fire going down, and by snow, which was landing gently on our faces. It was just starting. It was beautiful, and we sat up, and then stood up, but didn't say anything. We reeled in and checked our hooks, and found that the shrimp were gone again.

Kirby looked out at the darkness, where surely the snowflakes were landing on the water, and he looked up at the sky, and could not stand the beauty.

"I'm going to try to hitchhike back to Houston," he said. He did not say her name but I know he was thinking of waking up with Tricia, and looking out the window, and seeing the snow, and everything being warm, inside the house, under the roof.

"No," I said. "Wait." Then I was cruel. "You'll just get in a fight again," I told him, though I knew it wasn't true: they were always wild to see each other after any kind of separation, even a day or two. I had to admit I was somewhat jealous of this.

"Wait a little longer, and we'll go out into the waves," I said.

"Yes," said Kirby. "Okay." Because we'd been thinking that would be the best part, the most fun: wade-fishing. We'd read about that, too, and Kirby had brought a throw net, with which to catch mullets for bait.

We'd read about wade-fishermen with long stringers of fish— the really successful fishermen—being followed by sharks and attacked, and so we were pretty terrified of the sharks, knowing that they could be down there among our legs, in the darkness and under water, where we could not see, following us: or that we could even walk right into the sharks. That idea of them being hidden, just beneath us—we didn't like it a bit, not knowing for sure if they were out there or not.

We fixed a new batch of Cuba Libres, using a lot of lime. We stood at the shore in our waders, the snow and wind coming hard into our faces, and drank them quickly, strongly, and poured some more, raced them down. It wasn't ocean any more, but snowdrift prairie, the Missouri breaks, or the Dakotas and beyond, and we waded out, men searching for game, holding the heavy poles high over our heads, dragging the great Bible cast-nets behind us.

The water was not very deep for a long time; for fifteen minutes it was only knee-deep, getting no deeper, and not yet time to think about sharks.

"I wish Tricia was here," said Kirby. The Cuba Libres were warm in our bellies; we'd used a lot of rum in the last ones. "I wish she was riding on my shoulders, piggy-back," he said.

"Nekkid," I said.

"Yes," said Kirby, picturing it, and he was happy, and even though I didn't really like Tricia, I thought how nice it would have been if she could have seen him then, sort of looking off and dreaming about it. I wished I had a girlfriend or wife on my back, too, then, to go along with all the other equipment I was carrying. I was thinking that she could hold the pole, and cast out, waiting for a bite, waiting for the big fight; and I could work the throw net, trying to catch fresh mullet, which we'd cut up into cubes, right there in the water, and use for fresh bait: because the bait had to be fresh.

It was like a murder or a sin, cutting the live mullet's head off, slicing the entrails out, filleting out a piece of still-barely-living meat and putting it on the hook, and then throwing the rest of the mullet away; throwing it behind you for the sharks, or what-ever—head, fins, entrails, and left-over meat—casting your hook then far out into the waves and dark and snow, with that warm very fresh piece of flesh on the hook—it was like a sin, the worst of the animal kingdom, I thought, but if you caught what you were after, if you got the big redfish, then it was all right, it was possible that you were forgiven.

I wanted to catch the largest redfish in the world. I wanted to catch one so large that I'd have to wrestle it, maybe even stab it with the fillet knife, like Tarzan with the crocodiles.

Kirby looked tired. He had put on about twenty pounds since high school, and it was hard work, walking with the poles over our heads.

"Wait," I said. We stopped and caught our breath. It was hard to hear each other, with only the wind and waves around us; and except for the direction of the waves, splashing into our faces from the Gulf, we couldn't tell where shore was, or in which direction the ocean lay.

"I've an idea," said Kirby, still breathing heavily, looking back to where we were pretty sure the shore was. If our fire was still burning, we couldn't see it. "There's a place back up the beach that rents horses in the daytime. Some stables."

"They shoot horse thieves," I said. But I thought it was a wonderful idea. I was tired, too; I wasn't in as good of shape as I'd once been either.

"I'll go get them," I said, since I wasn't breathing quite as hard as he was. It was a tremendous picture: both of us on white horses, riding out into the waves, chest-deep, neck-deep, then the magic lift and float of the horse as it began to swim, the light feeling of nothing, no resistance.

Mares, they would be, noble and strong, capable of carrying foolish, drunken men out to sea on their journey, if they so desired, and capable of bringing them back again, too.

"Yes," I said. "You stay here. I'll go find the horses."

Back on shore, walking up the beach to the stables, I stopped at a pay phone, and dialed Tricia's number. The cold wind was rocking the little phone booth, and there was much static on the line.

"Tricia," I said, disguising my voice, mumbling. "This is Kirby. I love you." Then I hung up, and thought about how I really liked her after all, and I went to look for the horses. It would be perfect.

We could ride around out in the gulf on the swimming horses until they tired, casting and drinking, searching for what we were after, pausing sometimes to lean forward and whisper kind things, encouragement, into the horses' ears, as they labored through the waves, blowing hard through their nostrils, legs kicking and churning, swimming around in wide circles out in the gulf, in the darkness, the snow; no doubt full of their own fears of sharks, of drowning, of going down under too heavy of a load, and of all the things unseen, all the things below.